DISASTROUS SEPTEMBER

A Novel

SKIFTER KELLICI

Translated from the Albanian by

CARRIE HOOPER

First printing 2022.
ISBN 978-1-716-05067-1

Translator's Note: I am thankful to Anitta Muharremi for her work on this project.

In memory of the 2981 victims of the September 11, 2001 terrorist attacks on the World Trade Center, among them three Albanians: Frrok Camaj, Mon Gjonbalaj and Simon Dedvukaj.

CONTENTS

PART I: MAY 20, 2001 AROUND 9 AM

A long line of passengers waited to go through one of the Terminal B security checkpoints at Logan International Airport in Boston, Massachusetts. An alarm sounded as a middle-aged man went through the metal detector. He shrugged his shoulders with surprise and looked a little nervous. When the security employee asked him to walk through the metal detector again, he obeyed. The alarm went off a second time. Therefore, he ordered the passenger to lift his arms above his head and spread his legs, while he patted him down with a wand. A beep indicated an object in his jacket pocket. When the security employee asked the passenger to empty his pockets, he took out a small metal hammer. When the worker said he could not take the hammer on board, the passenger insisted it wasn't a weapon but a tool for carving small children's toys. The passenger's shouting drew the attention of the other passengers. A few minutes later, two police officers arrived and took him away. A medical examination confirmed he suffered from schizophrenia. After this incident, everything returned to normal, even though the passengers were slightly shaken by the scene.

Two men with cups in their hands, who didn't appear to be traveling anywhere, sat in the waiting area. They watched the passengers as they prepared to board their flights and paid particular attention to the metal objects they carried. They spoke in hushed tones.

"If we can make ourselves invisible and avoid getting caught like that idiot!" said Muhammad Ata, an Egyptian student.

"Don't worry," said his friend, Marvan al Shehin, a student from the United Arab Emirates. "We don't have to make ourselves invisible."

"Will we have weapons?!" Muhammad cried.

"Of course," said Marvan.

"What kind of weapons?"

Muhammad sounded concerned. Marvan didn't respond.

"Why don't you answer me?"

Marvan remained silent.

"You know a lot more than I do. You were close to Osama bin Laden, May God preserve him. You know all about these weapons. Why won't you tell me anything?"

"Because I don't know anything," said Marvan. "Only Osama and Khalid Sheikh Muhammad,

his right hand man, know about them. I can only imagine what they look like."

He smiled and reassured his friend everything would be fine.

"What matters is we will hijack the planes and wait for further instructions. This will be our greatest mission with Al Qaeda in the name of Allah!"

Muhammad remained silent. He admired Marvan because he knew Osama bin Laden who had taught him how to hijack a plane. At the same time, he was proud to participate in this important mission.

When Jacqueline Cramer, a young blond woman in her twenties, had reached the 107th floor at the top of one of New York's Twin Towers, and had backed into a corner, she retreated quickly. She felt dizzy and leaned against the rails. She looked down and saw part of Manhattan, the Statue of Liberty, part of New Jersey, and JFK Airport where she had often landed and boarded flights. She cried out in amazement, and her fiancé, Steve, standing behind her, marveled at her surprised.

"You're a flight attendant. You've flown higher than this."

"Yes, Honey, but a plane is an enclosed space with a controlled temperature. It's different up here. We're not on the ground, but we're not in the air, either. It feels really weird."

Besim Istrefi, the man in charge of cleaning the outer windows, said, "She's right. We're between heaven and earth. I've worked here for 25 years, and I still feel that way. On rainy days, I stay dry and soak up the sun."

Besim was tall with blue, laughing eyes and a bubbly personality. He took time to talk to this American couple, two of the many tourists who visited the Twin

Towers every day. Steve Ferguson, a reporter for CNN, had come to interview Besim and Marko, two Albanians in charge of cleaning the windows of this tall building from which one could see the entire city.

Jacqueline shivered.

"Do you regret climbing up here?" asked Besim, handing her a jacket. "It's always cold."

Jacqueline could only imagine what it was like in the winter.

"No," she said, as she put on the jacket. "The view is spectacular. Furthermore, I've never watched Steve at work. Since today is my day off, I decided to join him."

"She wants to steal my job," said Steve, winking at Besim.

"Oh no," said Jacqueline. "I'm more comfortable in a plane though I admit I feel like a caged bird. But I wouldn't trade the flights for anything, regardless of the risks. I can't wait to go back to Boston."

"I feel the same way about this place," said Besim. "I don't get to fly like you do, but I get to enjoy the view. Nobody else but me works at these heights, except you, of course."

"You window cleaners have a difficult and dangerous job," said Steve. "A few journalists have written articles about you, but readers need something more concrete, more pictures, so they have a better understanding of your work. That's why I decided to make a documentary. I want to finish the script as soon as possible. I think it's great that you, an Albanian from

Kosovo, and Marko Muzaka, an Arberesh, have this job. The documentary will be fascinating. If I'm not mistaken, the Arberesh are the Albanians who fled to Greece during the time of the Ottoman Empire."

"That's correct," said Besim. "They still speak Albanian and have preserved their traditions. You seem to know quite a bit about Albania."

"My father's friend went there on a mission right after World War II. He talked about it all the time. He told us how Albania gained its independence after centuries of Ottoman rule and how the SuperPowers gave land to its neighbors. For instance, they gave Kosovo to Serbia."

"Their dirty politics harmed my people," said Besim with a frown. "Kosovo remained autonomous even after Enver Hoxha gave it to Tito's Yugoslavia."

Besim's sad face moved Steve.

"We Kosovars knew Albanians had it bad, but we had it worse. The Serbs tortured us. Radio Tirana, which we listened to in secret, made everything seem wonderful. I learned the truth in the summer of 1968 when I fled to Albania. It's a long story I hope to tell you one day."

"My dad's friend had the same experience," said Steve. "During the first year of the Anglo-American missions in Albania, he saw how people were treated. He even witnessed the arrest and torture of a graduate of Tirana Technical School, built by Harry Fultz, an American who loved Albania. The man in question said Albania should be free like America."

Steve shrugged his shoulders with sadness.

"Since then, although I was young, I fell in love with Albania and learned more about it. I even told Jacqueline a few stories about it. Isn't that right, Jacqueline?"

She nodded.

"Thank you, Mr. Ferguson," said Besim, laying a hand gently on his shoulder. His eyes sparkled.

"I still don't see Marko Muzaka," said Steve.

He wanted to start the interview as soon as possible.

"I don't see him, either. He must be in the other tower. We usually don't need a phone to communicate. We just yell from here like two mountain dwellers from Kosovo or Albania. I hope he'll be here soon."

"Aren't your wife and children afraid for you, working so high up?" asked Jacqueline, her eyes open wide.

"Well," said Besim, "my first day here, I felt lightheaded and started having second thoughts about this job. I told myself, Besim, this job is not for you! My supervisor was watching me and said even though the job was dangerous, I would come to like it. And he was right. I was scared the first few weeks. As I cleaned the windows, I would see the employees in their offices, wearing shirts and suits, while I shivered in the strong wind, even with a heavy jacket. But as the days passed, I got used to the work and really started to like it."

Besim's honesty impressed Steve and Jacqueline.

"Did your wife know what you did?" asked Steve, holding a pen and a notebook.

"To tell you the truth, if Marta, my wife, an Albanian from Montenegro, had known I worked close to the clouds, she would never have approved."

"When did she find out about your job?" asked Jacqueline, pushing her hair from her face.

"I didn't tell her for almost two years. Where do you work, she would ask me. Where most Albanians work and get paid well, I would answer. She didn't object since I made quite a bit of money. But one day, after I got home from work, she handed me The Daily News."

"Oh, I read that article at the library and that's one of the reasons I wanted to make this documentary," Steve interrupted. "I copied it and read it over and over. I feel like I've known you for a long time. Fearing persecution by the Serbs, you fled from Kosovo to Albania, escaped to Greece, and emigrated to America. I'm going to include more details in my documentary."

"I never dreamed CNN would make a documentary about me," said Besim, surprised. He looked at Steve, then at Jacqueline.

"How would you feel if I interviewed Marta as well?" asked Steve.

"That would be great. I'll call her right away," said Besim.

He called Marta, who worked in a factory. She was surprised an American wanted to interview her.

Laughing, she said, "Well, Mr. Ferguson, I showed Besim a newspaper with a photo of him hanging out of a tall building which appeared to be made of lego blocks. I guess he never thought I'd see it and find out the truth."

"What happened next?" asked Steve.

"I yelled, First thing tomorrow morning, I want you to tell your supervisor you are quitting, you hear me! Besim said, I'm not quitting my job tomorrow or ever. We had a big fight and after he insisted he wasn't going to quit, I went to the Twin Towers. I wanted to watch him work."

"You went there?" said Steve.

"Before dawn, Mr. Ferguson, up to the 105th floor, and I saw him in that cage, washing the windows. I shouted, Oh my God, so this is where my poor husband works! I followed him down the stairs. It was a beautiful, sunny day, but suddenly, it got very windy and the cage started to shake like a small boat on a stormy sea. I was scared, but thankfully the wind didn't last long.

With the touch of a button, the cage stopped shaking and started to rise. Well, what do you think of my job? Besim asked. It's very dangerous, especially for someone in their fifties."

Marta was silent.

"Thank you," said Steve. "See you soon."

"See you soon," said Marta.

While Steve, Jacqueline, and Besim were talking, many people entered the first tower, among them, an Arab in his thirties named Jaser al-Sadri. He was thin and of average height, with thick, dark hair. He wore jeans and a blue coat. He approached a checkpoint similar to those at an airport, took his keys and some loose change out of his pockets, and put them in a bin, but as he passed through security, an alarm sounded.

"Please pass through again," said one of the guards.

Jaser walked through a second time, and the alarm sounded again.

"Did you leave anything in your pockets?"

Jaser shrugged his shoulders, checked his pockets, and removed a small knife. He smiled and said, "I forgot about this knife."

"It's larger than the maximum size allowed," said the guard.

"That's funny," said Jaser. "When I bought it, it looked just like the one I lost a few days ago. What should I do?"

"Leave it here. We'll give it back to you on your way out."

"Thank you," said Jaser as he left the knife with the guard and went through the security checkpoint again.

Jacqueline couldn't take her eyes off the cage which hoisted Besim up to the windows he needed to clean.

"May I go up with you?" she asked.

"No," said Besim. "I'm the only one allowed in here."

"I can't come with you either, not even during the interview?" Steve wondered.

Besim was quiet for a moment.

"I'm not sure, but I think we can work something out. My boss said Said, whom you met earlier, might be able to help you. He is a refugee from Algeria who came to America ten years ago. He is a good guy and a hard worker. He started working here five years ago as a regular employee. Then he became a supervisor, and now he is the company manager and a full time student. I think he can work something out."

Besim glanced at Steve.

"Besides, when Said sees what a lovely couple you and Jacqueline make, he won't hesitate to let you ride in the cage with me. Am I right, Jacqueline?"

"Absolutely," said Jacqueline with a smile. "I was hooked the moment I saw Steve's blue eyes. We met last September at a party at the Logan Airport Hilton in Boston. Steve had come to the airport to make a documentary."

Jacqueline looked back at Steve.

"Don't listen to her," said Steve. "She is exaggerating because she loves me."

"She's not exaggerating at all. She made the right decision when she chose you," said Besim.

"I chose her, too," said Steve, hugging Jacqueline.

A dark-haired man approached them.

"There's Marko Muzaka."

"I'm sorry I'm late," said Marko, shaking everyone's hand. "One of the visitors wasn't feeling well, so I had to help him to the elevator. I didn't have a chance to call you."

"I would forgive you any day but today when Steve Ferguson, one of the most famous CNN reporters, is visiting us here in New York," said Besim.

Marko looked at Steve.

"You're right, Besim," he said. "Ever since you showed me the photos of you in *The Daily News* and *The Times*, I hoped I, too, would receive that kind of publicity one day. I felt honored when RAI (Italian Radio and Television) made a documentary about the Arberesh in the village of Saint Miter in Corona, Italy where I was born and lived for a short time before my parents emigrated to America. I was very young when they recorded me singing an Arberesh song. The history of the Arberesh really moves me."

"I heard Arberesh songs are very beautiful," said Jacqueline.

"Yes. The song I sang as well as every other Albanian and Balkan song is beautiful."

"Can you sing that song now?" asked Jacqueline.

Steve was surprised by her "selfish" request, especially because they had just met. He wanted to tell her not to impose on Marko, but he stopped when he saw her request didn't bother him at all. He immediately started singing:

"Beautiful More,
How could I leave you
Never to see you again!
My God is there.
My mother is there.
My brother is there.
They are all buried there.
Beautiful More,
I'm speaking with tears in my eyes.

More, Arberi!"

Marko sang from the bottom of his heart. Even though they couldn't understand the words, Steve and Jacqueline could feel his nostalgia. Besim, who had heard the song hundreds of times and had taught it to his students, felt for the thousands of Albanians, who longed for their homeland.

"In order to escape the Ottomans, who wanted to enslave the Albanians in their own country, my ancestors emigrated to Morea in Peloponnese, Greece," said Marko. "When the Turks conquered that area, the Albanians moved to Calabria, Sicily, and other parts of southern Italy where this song, the symbol of the Arberesh, was "born." After the documentary aired on RAI, I felt like a king. Whenever they saw me, kids would shout, Good job, Marko! You sang that song beautifully! Now Besim and I are going to be on CNN."

"You are true heroes," said Steve. "That's why American journalists have taken an interest in you."

"I'm not a hero," said Besim. "I'm sure you remember what happened in this tower on February 23, 1993."

"Of course. I was in my last year at Columbia University, and I remember a documentary about a group of terrorists, who planted a bomb in the basement. There were a few casualties as well as damage to the building. The terrorists were later arrested."

"That's right." Besim nodded. "I was getting ready to clean the windows. It was around noon, and I felt a slight tremor. The lights in the offices went out, and the alarm sounded. I wondered what was going on. I looked down and saw a cloud of dust and smoke. I could hear people screaming for help. I knew my life was in danger, but I refused to give up. I decided to stay right where I was. Other workers stayed put, too. Later, I found out the elevators weren't working because the power had gone out. I just stood there and wondered what to do."

"What happened next?" asked Jacqueline.

"When I realized I was the only one up there, I went down the fire escape. It took four hours to get out. No one would have recognized me, not even my wife and kids. I was tired and scared, and my face was dirty from all the smoke. I never told Marta about the incident.

She wouldn't have let me work there anymore. No, Mr. Ferguson, I'm not a hero. I did what I had to do."

Steve and Jacqueline were awestruck.

"You had no choice," said Steve.

"You had to save yourself," added Jacqueline. "It would have been foolish to stay up there."

Besim felt somewhat relieved after hearing Jacqueline's words.

"I agree," said Marko. "Have you heard what George Willington did in 1977?"

Steve thought for a moment.

"Oh yeah," he said. "I read about him. I was only five when the incident you're referring to happened."

"Besim was 35," said Marko. "He had come to America the previous year."

"I've never heard of George Willington," said Jacqueline.

"Of course you haven't. You weren't even born yet," laughed Steve.

"Must you always remind me that you are older than me?" asked Jacqueline, playfully.

"Please, Besim, tell us what you saw," urged Steve.

"On a beautiful summer morning, around 7, I was getting ready to go to work in the south tower, when I saw a man climbing the North Tower, where Marko has been working for the past two years. He was holding a rope like a mountain climber."

"And nobody else saw him?" asked Jacqueline.

"Of course other people saw him," said Besim. "A few minutes later, the police, the fire department, and an ambulance came to the main entrance of the building. The police kept asking the man to come down slowly, but he wouldn't listen. They even put an inflatable platform under him, in case he fell. After almost five hours, he reached the top of the tower. He waved at me and said he had made it safe and sound. The police, firefighters, and doctors were already there. The man didn't appear to be crazy. In fact, he had a college degree."

"That's why I'm saying you would have been more stupid than Willington if you had stayed up there when the bomb exploded in the basement of the Towers," said Marko.

"You know what, a reporter from Boston said the same thing when

I told him the story," said Besim.

"Who?" asked Jacqueline.

"Sokol Kama, an Albanian journalist."

"Sokol Kama!" Steve exclaimed. "He's my friend. Jacqueline introduced us at Logan Airport."

"Really?" asked Besim. "Marko, you remember Sokol, don't you?"

"Of course. A framed copy of his interview hangs on my wall."

"Jacqueline, do you work with Sokol?" asked Besim.

"Yes," she said. "He is a security supervisor in Terminal B. To be honest, he doesn't belong there. He's a wonderful journalist and a talented writer. I've sent several of his books to schools in Kosovo and Albania. One night at the airport, he told me all about Communist Albania. I'm sure you've heard about that, Steve?"

"I hear news about the political situation in Kosovo and Albania every day," said Steve."

"Last year, Sokol did a report similar to one by some American journalists here in New York," said Jacqueline. "I'll give him a call right now and tell him where we are."

"He'll be so surprised," said
Besim with a smile.

The long Terminal B corridor was filled with passengers, and one could see the sunset through the windows. Sokol Kama was occupied with a passenger who set off the alarm several times even though he had emptied his pockets. After a few attempts to pass through security, he became a little annoyed and said there shouldn't have been any problem since he had removed everything from his pockets. Sokol told him he had to pat down his body with a magnetic wand. As soon as the wand touched his torso, the alarm sounded again.

"Can you please lift up your shirt?" asked Sokol, and the passenger obeyed. "You should have taken off your belt, sir."

"Why would I do that?" asked the passenger. "It's not metal!"

"It's just a precaution. There's a piece of metal there. We don't want anyone bringing weapons on the plane."

"I wouldn't do that, and I'm sure with all this security, not even the craziest terrorist would do that," said the old man, smiling.

"George!" a woman shouted. "Stop fooling around. The man is right. It's true you're not hiding anything, but someone else could be, and God knows what would happen to the passengers or the pilot if a person with concealed weapons got on the plane."

"For God's sake, Amanda, why are you lecturing me? Things like that don't happen anymore, especially in this airport."

"Regardless, it's our job to keep the passengers and employees safe," said Sokol.

"He knows that," said Amanda. "He just likes to joke with people. Don't mind him, sir. You do whatever's necessary to keep everybody safe."

Just then, Sokol's phone rang, and he answered it.

"Hello, Sokol. It's Jacqueline."

"Where are you? In New York?"

"Yes. As a matter of fact, I'm calling you from the highest point in the city."

"The Twin Towers?"

"That's right."

"What in the world are you doing there? By chance, did you and Steve have a fight, and now you want to kill yourself right before your wedding?"

"I wouldn't do that if his life depended on it," laughed Jacqueline.

"Ah, love is strange," said Sokol. "Are you two visiting the Twin Towers?"

"No," said Jacqueline. "Steve is working on a documentary, and I'm keeping him company."

"That's great. I wrote an article about the people who clean the windows when I was in New York last year."

"You wrote about some Albanians who work on the 107th floor where we are!"

"How did you know?"

"I'm with one of them right now. Here, talk to him."

A few seconds later, a deep male voice said, "Sokol, do you remember me?"

"Of course. Besim Istrefi! In our profession, you remember every voice of every person you've interviewed."

"Well, Steve is making a documentary about me and Marko Muzaka, an Arberesh whose family history you found fascinating. We're going to be on TV."

Steve told Sokol how happy he was when Besim told him

about Sokol's article about Albanians in the States.

"They deserve that kind of recognition," said Sokol. "And who better than you to tell their story."

"I'm going to mention you on camera," said Marko. "I'll talk about the article you wrote last year."

Sokol laughed.

"We won't keep you any longer since you're at work and probably very busy," said Jacqueline. "I'll see you in two days at the airport. Bye-bye."

Sokol was in shock. Never in a million years had he expected to talk to Besim on the phone from the same tower where he had interviewed him a year ago. The fact Jacqueline and Steve were also there was remarkable, too.

"Be careful, Sokol. People from the Federal Aviation Administration will show up when we least expect them, and you know how they are. They can't wait to find mistakes," said Gary Minke, a short, middle-aged man and the head of Capital Security, the company for which Sokol worked. It was hard to tell from the way he spoke if his words were meant as advice, a threat, or both.

"Don't stay on the phone too long," he continued, coming closer to Sokol. "And one more thing, you need to be more friendly with the passengers, even if they're wrong, like the last passenger. Anyone who complains is right as far as we're concerned."

After his lecture, he ran from the checkpoint without giving Sokol the chance to explain himself. Sokol wanted to follow him. This was not the first time Gary had acted this way. He took his lunch break early in order to regain his composure. As he was going to get a cup of coffee, he saw his friend, Fatie Bashri, a petite, twenty-year-old woman from Afghanistan, who spoke broken English. She had started working at the airport the previous year. Sokol told her about his encounter with Gary.

"He doesn't care what we do," said Fatie. "Even if we work hard and do a good job, he won't pay us more than eight dollars an hour. If you don't like it, leave. A lot of people are looking for work. That's Gary's favorite sentence. Nothing else matters as long as his company makes money. That's why he makes a big deal about the FAA."

Sokol and Fatie sat at a table.

"I just talked to Jacqueline," said Sokol as he sipped his coffee. "She was in one of the Twin Towers!"

"Where your Albanian friends work, the ones you wrote about?"

"Yes. Steve, Jacqueline's fiancé, was there, too."

He told Fatie about Steve's documentary and their telephone conversation.

"The documentary he made last September about the airport was amazing," she said.

Sokol nodded.

"I remember he interviewed both you and Jacqueline."

She winked at him.

"That's when Steve's and Jacqueline's romance started," Sokol said with a smile. "Do you remember how happy and in love they looked that night at the Hilton when they danced to *Come Back in September*?"

Sokol sang slowly:

"Honey, come back in September,
The month we met.
Come back so we can hold hands again."

"It's a beautiful love song," said Fatie.

"I'm excited Steve is making a documentary about my two Albanian friends and is focusing on Besim Istrefi," said Sokol.

"Is that the man from Kosovo who fled to Albania and later came to America?"

Fatie had learned a little about Albania and Albanians from the stories Sokol had told her, mostly during their breaks.

Sokol nodded.

"He was not allowed to set foot in Yugoslavia, more specifically, in

Kosovo. If he had done so, he would have been executed. His uncle was arrested for speaking out against the regime. At that time, the people, who had lived under Serbian rule for decades, wanted Kosovo to become a republic and demanded more rights and freedoms. They pleaded for the right to study in their own language and to raise their own flag. When Besim realized he was in danger of being arrested like his uncle, he left his hometown of Prizren and escaped to nearby Albania. He carried a pistol. The Serbian guards spotted him as he was crossing the border and shouted for him to surrender."

Sokol paused, trying to remember every detail. Fatie listened intently, eager to hear the rest of the story.

Sokol continued: "Besim did not obey the guards' order to stop. He knew if he had, he would have suffered the same fate as his uncle. The guards would have arrested him and beaten him to death. Although he was exhausted, he continued to run through the bushes until he reached Albania. Then, he knelt down and kissed the ground. he was bleeding profusely and realized he had been shot in the shoulder. He surrendered to the Albanian border guards, who tended to his wounds. Since he was a teacher, they offered him a job in Berat, a town in southern Albania. After a few months, however, he and other refugees from Kosovo sensed they were being watched and could be arrested or worse. Besim realized the Albanian regime was similar to, if not worse, than the one in Kosovo. The UDB had agreed to arrest any Albanians who crossed the border illegally. Because of this dirty game, Albanians were divided between two states. Besim learned that one of his friends was offered "a job" in another town in Albania, but in fact, he was deported to Yugoslavia and was killed on the way there. He was left somewhere in the mountains."

"Did Besim get out of Albania?"

"He told me his friend asked some of his friends from the Folklore

Institute to take him on an expedition in some small villages. He had gone on expeditions with them before. One stormy night, he decided to escape to Greece. As he approached the border, he heard footsteps. It's the Border Patrol, he thought. They've caught me! He hid behind some thick bushes, and indeed, the border guards passed right in front of him. Years ago, when he was wounded as he crossed into Albania, the guards had saved his life. Now circumstances had changed. A guard shouted, Don't let him get away! That dog is our enemy! We want him dead or alive! Besim considered surrendering and telling the guards he loved his country as much as they did, the country from which he had been forced to flee and now felt he had betrayed. But he forced himself to keep going. It's awful to leave your country. Besim stayed in a small town for a few months until the US approved his request to emigrate there. He didn't know what kind of work he could get so he decided to become a window cleaner at the Twin Towers. But his heart was still in Kosovo."

"Didn't he try to go back to Kosovo in 1999?" asked Fatie.

"Yes. He came here with the hope of one day returning home for good."

Sokol emphasized the last few words, as if he himself had experienced this sad adventure. Then, changing the subject, he asked, "What about you? Any news from your family in Afghanistan?"

A look of sadness crossed Fatie's face.

"A family friend who moved from Afghanistan to Pakistan and now lives in Karachi said the Taliban torture people who disobey the rules, even people in remote villages. They murder men, women, and children. They are animals."

Sokol remembered the first day he had seen Fatie. The many horrors she had lived through had scarred her soul, and she had looked terrified. Sokol learned what had happened to her and her four friends in the small Afghan village where they had been born and raised. They wanted to go to school, read more than the Koran, and hang out with their friends. They opposed wearing the burka. In short, they wanted the freedom to be themselves. When the Taliban found out, they were outraged, searched for them everywhere, and wanted to burn them alive in public. But the villagers hid them. The Taliban killed Fatie's family since they couldn't find her or her friends. A villager helped the girls escape to another village where the residents sheltered them, cared for them, and fed them. They moved from one village to another with the Taliban in hot pursuit. One day, as the girls were running toward the International Red Cross building, the Taliban shot and killed three of them. Fatie and a friend survived and came to America.

"I don't understand why men in their twenties embrace the Taliban's warped beliefs," said Sokol. "I was shocked to read they are proud to die for their cause."

"They are fanatics," sighed Fatie. "They don't recognize any book but the Koran, and they read a special edition, given to them by Osama bin

Laden. Conditions in Afghanistan worsened once he arrived in 1996. When my friend and I were in hiding, we heard the villagers say bin Laden and his friends from Al Qaeda wandered through the area. He made our lives miserable, and I'm sure he will continue to wreak havoc in America because according to him, the countries in the West, especially the United States, are Islam's greatest enemies. But he will probably be killed one day. Don't you agree?"

"I don't know. But one thing is certain: bin Laden and Al Qaeda pose the greatest threat to the world. We are in danger every minute, especially here where we work."

Fatie shivered and felt bin Laden's presence, even in the airport.

"Are you cold, Honey?" Steve asked Jacqueline as she buttoned up the jacket Besim had given her.

"Only you can warm me up," she laughed.

"Even I, who am used to working in the cold, am a little chilly today," said Besim. "Let's go to Said's office. He's waiting for us."

"Okay," said Steve. "Now I know how high up you work."

"When you get in that cage, and the wind rocks it like a cradle, you'll really get a feel for these heights," said Marko. "To tell you the truth, I get scared up there."

"That doesn't mean Steve will be," said Besim.

"I'll let you know how I felt once I've done it," said Steve, looking at Jacqueline.

The group reached the elevator that would take them to Said's office on the 50th floor. When it stopped on the 64th floor, an older man got in.

"That's Rrok Cemi," said Besim. "Another Albanian who works for this company."

"Does he work in the Towers?" asked Steve.

"No," said Rrok. "I'm not as brave as Marko and Besim. I'm a mechanic on the lower floors."

"Everyone chooses the job they like best," said Steve, when Rrok seemed a little uncomfortable.

"The night of November 28, 1989, a group of us gathered in a New York hotel to celebrate our Independence Day, and Rrok introduced me to Marta, his niece, my future wife," said Besim. "I was almost 50 years old, but better late than never, right? We liked each other, and soon we got married. We have a son named Trim (which means brave)."

"How many kids do you have," Jacqueline asked Rrok.

Rrok hesitated for a moment.

"He never got married," said Besim.

Steve looked at Jacqueline, as if he wanted to tell her not to ask too many personal questions.

"Such is life," said Rrok.

"Aren't you from Montenegro like Besim's wife," asked Jacqueline.

Rrok nodded.

"My wife is a Christian, and I am a Muslim," said Besim.

"At one time, mixed marriages were not allowed because they violated the teachings of the Koran," said Steve. "Fanatics still don't approve of them."

"Religion never caused us any problems," said Rrok. "Especially nowadays. We come from the same place, speak the same language, and share the same blood. That's all that matters."

Steve was amazed.

"I read that Albanian Muslims are different from Islamic extremists," he said. "This shows how noble the Albanians are. Other nations still suffer from this social plague."

"If religion mattered, the Albanians wouldn't survive. The three main religions in Albania are Islam, Catholicism, and Orthodoxy," Besim explained.

"I witnessed this religious tolerance when I visited Albania for the first time," said Marko. "I was amazed."

They had reached the 25th floor.

"I have to get back to work," said Rrok. "I can't wait to see your documentary on CNN."

He said good-bye and left.

"Rrok could retire, but he likes his job. He will continue to work until we decide to return home," said Besim.

"I want to keep working, too," said Steve.

As they walked along, Said Akbar, a young man with curly hair and spiffy clothes, which contrasted nicely with his dark skin, greeted them.

"I'd like to interview you, Mr. Akbar," said Steve."

"I can't be part of your documentary," said Said, "because I give Besim and Marko orders from the comfort of my office, not from the cage they work in on the 107th floor."

"I understand," said Steve, "but Besim told us how you rose in this company, and that's absolutely remarkable. Therefore, you belong in the documentary."

"Then let's go to the restaurant," said Said.

The sun shone through the windows and reached the table where Steve, Jacqueline, Besim, Marko, and Said were sitting.

"Two years ago, you married an American you met in this building?" Steve asked.

Said nodded, smiled, and showed his white teeth which made him more attractive.

"Serena and I will be parents in September."

"Oh, Jacqueline and I are getting married on September 16!" Steve almost shouted.

"Perhaps our child will be born the same day," said Said.

Jacqueline and Steve looked at each other, as if they were trying to tell each other something.

"What about you, Besim? Do you have any plans for September?" asked Jacqueline.

"I'll be retiring and moving back to Kosovo with my wife and son," he said. "And so is Rrok."

Steve and Jacqueline were surprised to hear this.

"But you've lived here for many years," said Jacqueline. "You're

Americans now. You work and have a family. Why do you want to leave?"

"There's an old Albanian proverb: A stone longs for its country," said Besim, his voice breaking. "We, the rocks of our country, long for our homeland."

After a brief pause, he continued: "Two years ago, in 1999, the so-called butcher Milloshevìq sent Serbian troops to Kosovo to kill as many Albanians as possible. Indeed, they killed many, and over a million were forced to leave. I dreamed of returning to my birthplace. I joined the Kosovo Liberation Army shortly after its formation."

"The Serbs massacred Albanian civilians," said Steve.

Besim shook his head in pain.

"I told my wife and son, I will come for you as soon as we liberate Kosovo. I returned to my homeland to join the other young people in the Liberation Army, and I remembered a poem written in 1937 by the well-known Albanian poet, Esat Mekuli. At that time, the Serbian publicist, Cubrillovic, wrote a memorandum in which he demanded that Albanians from Kosovo be sent to Turkey. I translated Esat Mekuli's poem into English."

Besim closed his eyes, as if trying to remember the poem, then recited:

"Can you blame Albanians
For wanting to live in their country
Until the end of time?!
Is it a crime Albanians still stand
Under Mother Kosovo's sky
In the land of their ancestors
Despite their pain?!"

This profound poem touched Steve and Jacqueline.

Besim continued: "One day, other soldiers and I learned that Serbian paramilitary forces had captured several women, children, and elderly people and planned to burn them alive in a nearby stable. We arrived just as they were about to massacre unarmed civilians. We could hear women and children screaming. During the fighting, I got shot, just as I had when I fled to Albania, and almost fell into the arms of the people who had sentenced me to death in my absence. Some villagers rescued me and helped me cross the border into Macedonia. Though wounded, I managed to board an American military jet which had been sent to bring us Albanian-Americans back to the States temporarily."

Jacqueline felt sorry for Besim.

"Thanks to an ultimatum issued by President Bill Clinton as well as the NATO bombings, the Serbs were forced to leave Kosovo," said Besim. "Now that peace has returned, I see no reason for my family and me to stay here even though I call America my second home."

"YOU'RE right," said Jacqueline. "We Americans tend to forget that our ancestors, like you, came here for a better life."

"My parents, who are Arberesh, came here 40 years ago and are considered new immigrants," said Marko.

His words made Steve smile.

"Jacqueline and Marko are right. Take me, for example. The Fergusons came here over a century ago from the rocky mountains of Scotland, but I have never been there. I don't know if any of my relatives still live there. What about you, Jacqueline? Do you know anything about your German heritage?"

Jacqueline shrugged her shoulders with guilt.

"No. There are many Kramers in Bavaria in southern Germany, but I don't know if they are related to us. No one in my family speaks German."

"I give Besim, Rrok, and Sokol a lot of credit for wanting to go back to their homeland," said Steve. "Unlike us, they were born and raised there so they have many memories of their country."

"America is beautiful, and people can earn good money here," said Marko, "but I can't wait to go back to Italy."

"So you can marry a beautiful Arberesh girl," joked Besim.

"Exactly. Last year, during a visit to my hometown of San Demetrio, I met a girl, and she's coming to visit her family in September."

Steve's eyes widened, and he said, "There's a lot going on in September besides our wedding. Said and Serena are expecting their first child. Besim and Rrok are going home. Marko is getting married. Wouldn't it be nice to invite them to our wedding?"

Jacqueline jumped for joy and hugged Steve.

"That's a wonderful idea!" she said. "Will you come to our wedding?"

"Of course," said Besim. "We are honored to be part of this celebration. You're a wonderful couple."

"I'd like to invite another friend of yours," said Steve. "Can you guess who?"

"Sokol Kama," said Jacqueline. "That means we'll have lots of Albanians."

While they were talking, a man approached their table.

"That's Jaser al-Sadri," said Said. "He works for our company, too."

Jaser nodded to everyone.

"Jaser, like the rest of us, came to America a few years ago, and it looks like he'll work his way up in the company," said Said.

"Don't exaggerate," said Jaser. "Said is a different breed."

"Don't talk like that," said Said. "Anything is possible with hard work."

"Are you from Algeria, too," asked Steve.

"No, I'm from Lebanon. But we consider ourselves brothers since we're both Arabs and speak the same language."

Jaser's voice was calm.

"I heard Lebanon is a beautiful country with magnificent beaches that attract more and more tourists every year," said Jacqueline.

"That used to be the case, but not anymore," said Steve. "Religious differences have led to riots."

"Supported by nonreligious Americans," Jaser thought.

"We're trying to decide where to go for our honeymoon," said Jacqueline. "It's too bad there's so much trouble in Lebanon. It would have been nice to visit those beautiful beaches."

"If you're looking for beautiful beaches, you should go to southern Albania and visit costal towns like Saranda or Dhermi," said Marko.

Steve looked at him.

"Don't look so surprised, Mr. Ferguson. I went to Albania a few years ago and can tell you those are some of the most beautiful beaches on earth. Actually, I didn't go to Albania to frequent the beaches. I went to search for relatives and learned a lot about my family. I found records dating back to the 15th century. My family was scattered throughout southern Albania, in Berat and Saranda as well as parts of Greece and Italy. That's why I went to Saranda, a very old city with pristine beaches and a beautiful castle facing the sea."

"That's wonderful," said Said. "If you went to Algeria, you'd see beautiful beaches there as well. Steve, you and Jacqueline could spend your honeymoon in Algeria."

"Marko described the beaches of Albania as beautifully as a poet, and I love how the mountains meet the sea. As I told Besim, I've heard about Albania since I was little. Hey, Jacqueline, why don't we go to Albania for our honeymoon?"

"You won't regret it," said Besim.

"Honey, if you want to go to Albania, we can," said Jacqueline. "Sokol will be happy to hear we have decided to visit a beach in his country."

She and Steve embraced warmly, then left the restaurant. They could still see the sunset, now concealed by the tall building. They saw a beautiful young woman with short hair, coming out of the elevator.

"That's my wife, Serena Jackson," said Said.

Serena smiled and nodded.

"Said, you called me and told me to come to your office since Steve Ferguson was meeting you there. I've watched him on TV for years so I'm happy to meet him and his fiancé in person," she said, shaking Steve's and Jacqueline's hands.

"I forgot to tell you we were meeting in the restaurant," said Said.

Marko looked at Said and Serena.

"I didn't think there was another couple like Steve and Jacqueline, but now that I see Said and Serena, I'm not so sure. What do you think, my dear friends?"

"Marko never met Serena before?" said Jaser. "Even though she works here?"

"About 20 thousand people work in this building for more than 350 companies," said Serena. "I had never heard of Marko before even though he works with Said. Anyway, thank you for your kind words, Marko."

"Said and Serena make a nice couple indeed," thought Jaser. "He is a devoted Muslim who prays several times a day every day, and he married an American who wears a big, gold cross on a chain around her neck, like the ones Christians used to wear in Europe when they occupied the Islamic territories."

Jaser resented Said for marrying a Christian and was also jealous because Said quickly became a company manager who would likely receive a promotion soon.

"I hate you, Said, even though you've helped me and consider me a Muslim brother," thought Jaser. "I hate you even though you got me this job and always encourage me to do better. I hate you as much as I hate Americans, and I am ready to do what it takes to harm them. Allah, I can't wait to take revenge in your name!"

Lost in thought, Jaser jumped to his feet and said, "I'm sorry. I have to make a phone call."

He walked to a corner and took out his cell phone.

"Marvan, it's Jaser al-Sadri. Where are you?"

"At Terminal B in Logan Airport in Boston. I'm here with Muhammad Ata."

He moved to an area with fewer people.

"What happened?" he asked.

"A few minutes ago, I tried to go through security with a large knife, the one I use at work," said Jaser, "but the guard caught me."

"That's okay. What matters is we're doing our sacred duty. I can't explain it, but as I was talking with some infidels in the restaurant, I felt a lump in my throat."

"Why, Brother Jaser?"

"Get this, my manager, a Muslim from Algeria, is proud he married an American Christian. I can barely contain myself, especially since an American journalist from CNN is there with his fiancé and two other Albanians."

"Stay cool. Like I said, I'm here at the airport with Muhammad Ata to find out what people are allowed to take on board. Our holy day is near."

"Thank you, Brother Marvan."

When Jaser returned, everyone had left the restaurant, and people were walking toward the elevators.

"I've chosen most of the people for my documentary," Steve told Besim. "I'd like to meet Marta and Trim."

"Come anytime," said Besim. "Albanians are known for their hospitality."

"I will," said Steve.

"I can't wait to tell Marta who's coming to see us."

A song from over a century ago came through loud and clear on Radio Tirana, a station for immigrants. Marta had often heard it when she was growing up in Selishta, a village in Gruda. The song told the story of a brave warrior from Shkoder, Oso Kuka, and his 24 friends who killed Macedonians until they ran out of ammunition. When the Macedonian commander captured them in Vranina and ordered them to surrender, they refused and set barrels of gunpowder on fire, sacrificing their lives. The song moved Marta every time she heard it. She sang along with the radio and didn't realize Trim was listening.

"Mom, you sing beautifully," he said as he walked to the sofa where Marta sat. He was only 10 but very mature for his age. He had curly hair like his mother.

"This song brings back fond memories," said Marta.

"I know," said Trim. "You told me about Oso Kuka and the other brave men who fought with him."

"This song was written and performed in Shkoder as soon as the residents of the city learned of the bravery of Oso Kuka and his friends. It became very popular which infuriated the Montenegrans. You see, the world's leading countries took Gruda and other regions from Albania and gave them to Montenegro just like they gave Kosovo to Serbia. Your father has told you about these events which changed the lives of many Albanians."

Trim nodded. He had gained a deeper understanding of the tragedies which had forced his parents and thousands of other Albanians to flee their country. Marta continued:

"A hundred years ago, foreigners with their own maps invaded our country. In London in 1913, diplomats established Albania's new borders without considering the people who had lived there for centuries. Their decision separated families and neighbors. How was it possible that one village belonged to Albania, but the neighboring village belonged to Montenegro?"

Marta also told Trim about his great-grandfather, who was 20 years old at the time and had just gotten married.

"People married young back then," she said. "He was a construction worker, hired by the foreigners to build the new border crossings which were supposed to look like pyramids. He and his colleague built the pyramids, but in such a way that they would fall apart. If they didn't fall apart on their own, the workers would tear them down at night. The foreigners didn't know what was happening until one night, they caught your great-grandfather and his friends. They shot and killed your great-grandfather. His wife was pregnant with my father at the time. Those were hard times for

the people of Gruda. The Montenegrans, like the Serbs, persecuted Albanians and did everything in their power to force them out of their own country. Many people left Gruda and built a new village near Shkoder which they named New Gruda. The people who stayed in Gruda hoped things would change for the better, but they got worse. The Montenegrans killed my maternal grandparents. So we decided to emigrate to the United States, along with Rrok's family. We live in New York, but our hearts live in the old country to which we hope to return one day."

The phone rang, and Marta answered it. It was Besim. Marta's face glowed when she heard his cheerful voice.

"If you and Marko are going to be part of Steve's documentary, why do you need Trim and me?" she wondered.

Trim asked if an American journalist was making a documentary about their family.

"Yes, and he even invited us to his wedding," said Marta.

After she hung up the phone, she told Trim about the American his father had met at the Twin Towers.

Darkness had fallen, and Terminal B swarmed with passengers, waiting to board their flights. Sokol Kama felt tired so at 6 PM, he and Fatie decided to go home. Fatie lived in Dorchester, a suburb of Boston.

Sokol offered her a ride since it was on the way to Quincy where he lived. They were about to leave when out of nowhere, Gary appeared.

"You're leaving already, and at the busiest time of day?" he asked.

"We've been here since 5 this morning, a total of 13 hours," said Sokol. "Tomorrow we will do it again."

"I know," said Gary. "But don't you realize that if you go home now, that leaves just eight security personel?"

"That's how many there normally are," said Fatie.

"I know, but the airline managers have been complaining more and more lately. They want at least ten at each checkpoint, so please, can you stay for another hour? At least finish with the British Airways passengers. That manager complains the most."

Sokol and Fatie stole a quick glance at each other.

"You'll earn five hours overtime just for today. Imagine if you worked overtime every day! If you work another hour, I'll write off two. What do you say?"

"Mr. Minke, we work because we need the money," said Sokol. "We have to pay the rent and other bills. Everything is expensive nowadays."

"That's why I'm telling you to work."

"We are," said Fatie, "but we need a break sometimes. A few minutes ago, I almost fell asleep standing up."

"I understand," said Gary, "but just for today, work one more hour."

"Then we want a raise," said Sokol. "You know we have a difficult job. We have to stay alert. People quit every day simply because they are overworked and underpaid."

Gary forced a smile.

"Last year, I increased your pay from $7 to $8 an hour. All I'm asking is for you to stay one more hour. I will pay you double."

Sokol and Fatie decided to stay an extra hour.

"Did you hear him, Fatie? Double!"

"Like he's going to pay us out of his own pocket. He charges the company $18 an hour, and we only make $8 an hour. I can't get another job even if I wanted to. I just came to the US, and my English is not that good. It's different for you. You're a journalist so your

English is especially good, much better than mine. You could get another job."

Sokol nodded. They could not talk anymore because of the long line of passengers leaving for London. Fatie examined each bag on her screen, careful not to miss anything suspicious. Sokol stood by the conveyor belt. As a passenger in a beige

suit put his bag on the belt, an alarm sounded. By now, Fatie understood the system. Gray indicated regular items while blue indicated metal objects. She paid particular attention to the metal items as they could be weapons. She saw a metal object in the passenger's bag but was not sure if it was a small knife. She called Sokol over and asked him to check the bag. Fatie pointed to the metal object on the screen.

"I think it's a rather long knife," said Sokol.

As the passenger prepared to pick up his bag, Sokol asked to see it. The passenger seemed a little surprised but said, "Of course."

Sokol reached into the bag and found a beautiful, handcrafted silver knife in a box.

"This is a special knife, a gift for my friend in London," said the passenger with a smile. "I don't think it poses any danger."

Sokol closed his eyes and said, "I'm afraid it does. This is no ordinary knife, but it's a knife, and is longer than the maximum size allowed."

"But look at it. It's so dull you couldn't cut a piece of bread with it let alone kill someone."

This was not the first time Sokol had had to deal with this kind of problem and this type of passenger.

"You're right. This knife poses no danger, but as I'm sure you know, the FAA considers it a dangerous object. Even toys which look like weapons are prohibited, since they can cause confusion."

"Toys?"

"Yes, Sir. You can't tell the difference between toy weapons and real ones. It's a precaution. In some cases, terrorists have threatened passengers, pilots, and flight attendants with toy guns."

"Then what should I do?"

"Go to the person who checked your bag, tell them about the

knife, and fill out a form. As soon as you land in London and turn in the form, your bag and knife will be returned to you."

"All this fuss over a knife!" said the passenger, annoyed. He did not like the idea of having to go back to where he had checked his luggage. Meanwhile, the line of passengers grew longer and longer.

"When I come back, do I have to go through security again?" asked the passenger, looking at the other passengers who by this time had grown tired of waiting.

"We'll recheck you as soon as you come back."

"You have to recheck my bag!" said the passenger, surprised.

"Yes, sir. This is the last checkpoint before you board the aircraft."

"Why do you have to recheck me?"

"Because, sir, you could go back, get a weapon, and board the plane. Therefore, you have to go through screening again."

The passenger was about to say something else but changed his mind and left the checkpoint. Sokol breathed a sigh of relief. He looked at Fatie who couldn't wait to finish her shift. She was so tired she could hardly keep her eyes open. Suddenly, she spotted a small gun in one of the bags she was screening. It must be a toy, she thought, remembering Sokol's conversation with a passenger, but out of curiosity, she stopped the conveyor belt.

"Screen check!" she called. She was simply following the rules. Sokol came and looked at the screen.

"This can't be a gun," he said, "but I'll check it anyway."

Just then, someone called out, "Congratulations!", reached into his pocket, and took out a badge.

"My name is Jay Clement. I'm an FAA inspector. You did great. This was a test, and you passed. Could you tell me your name, please?"

"Fatie Bashri," said Fatie.

She could hear her heart pounding. The redheaded inspector removed a small book from his pocket and wrote down her name.

"I want to congratulate you again," he said. Then turning to Sokol, he said, "I want to congratulate you, too. You did a great job and you both were very attentive. You are good employees, and we are happy to know we have people like you taking care of our passengers and protecting the public from even the most skilled terrorists."

As Jay was writing Sokol's and Fatie's names in his book, Gary joined them.

"Congratulations, Fatie," he said, shaking her hand. "You'll get $25 from me and $25 from British Airways for your good work. $50 is nothing to sneeze at."

Fatie was happy, and Sokol smiled. He was proud of her. Fatie, however, didn't think she had done anything extraordinary. She was simply doing her job.

"It's time the FAA change its regulations," said Sokol.

Jay Clement was listening and said, "I don't understand. You mean you want to change the regulations followed at all airports nationwide?"

Sokol and Jay stepped aside so other passengers could get through.

"First of all, I think small objects like scissors and pocket knives should be prohibited since they are dangerous," said Sokol.

"You think they're dangerous?" asked Jay.

"Yes," said Sokol.

"I agree objects like the hammer, carried by an earlier passenger, shouldn't be allowed under any circumstances, but how could a pocket knife, shorter than 2 inches, pose any danger? It can't cut through a person's heart."

"Maybe not a person's heart, but certainly a person's throat."

The inspector laughed and said, "I appreciate your concern, but I can't say I agree with you. Terrorists have never used small objects as weapons and if they did, they would fail. Anyone could fight a small weapon. For instance, if an older person or aflight attendant saw a passenger with a small pocket knife, they could easily grab it from the assailant, and even if they couldn't, they would only get scratched, no big deal. The passenger would be caught immediately. Who would hijack a plane with an object the size of a finger? That will never happen. Do you have any other suggestions?"

Sokol heard the arrogance and sarcasm in Jay's voice.

"My colleagues and I also think passengers should take off their shoes and put them on the conveyor belt."

"Take off their shoes!" Jay cried. "But why?"

"Because small knives fit in a thick sole."

"Walking with a knife in one's shoe would be virtually impossible."

"But terrorists could carry explosives in their shoes."

"And do what? Blow themselves up with the plane?"

"I think glass bottles and perfumes should be prohibited as well."

"What's wrong with them?"

"Terrorists could break them, use them as weapons, or fill them with different types of gases."

Jay looked at Sokol.

"You may be right about glass bottles, but not about perfume bottles. Anyway, I appreciate your suggestions and will discuss them with my superiors."

"I appreciate that."

As soon as Jay left, someone tapped Sokol on the shoulder. At first, he thought it was a passenger, but when he turned around, he was surprised to see Gary.

"I overheard part of your conversation with Jay," he said. "Why in the world did you make those suggestions: no small knives, no bottles, not this, not that? Do you think you're smarter than the people who make the rules? Let me be clear: do your job and follow the rules. Nothing more. Do you understand?"

"What if the terrorists hijack a plane with the items I mentioned?"

"Sokol, please, just do your job and pay attention like Fatie. Don't make people like Jay come and test you on small objects which could be used as weapons because, thank God, that doesn't happen often. Be careful. You don't want to lose your job, right? If that happened, I couldn't help you. Besides, a lot of people are looking for this kind of work and are willing to work for less than eight dollars an hour. I repeat, follow the rules. The rest is of no concern to you."

Gary wanted to say more, but Sokol stopped him.

"Mr. Minke, you asked me to work an extra hour, and I've been here over an hour. I'm very tired and would like to leave. If you have anything else to tell me, I'll be back here at five AM tomorrow. Good night."

Gary approached Fatie and insisted she stay another hour. Of course, he told her, she would get paid double.

Sokol saw her nod in agreement even though she was as tired as he was.

Marvan and Muhammad had spent more than two hours at the Terminal B security checkpoint and had paid close attention to everything that had happened, including Sokol's conversation with the passenger. As they walked to the bus station, Marvan said, "As you can see, the trick is to get through security."

"You're right," said Muhammad. "When I was in Hamburg, I saw a documentary about the Greek mythological creatures, Cilla and Charybdis. Have you heard of them?"

"No," said Marvan.

"They were two sea monsters, and when ships sailed between them, they killed a lot of sailors. When we go through security, we have to stay calm so we don't suffer the same fate they did."

Marvan put a hand on Muhammad's shoulder.

"Don't worry," he said. "When that blessed day comes, we'll make it through security, and we won't suffer the fate of those sailors. As I told you before, this is your most important job so far."

"Thank you again for choosing me," said Muhammad, looking at Marvan in awe.

Sokol said good-bye to Fatie. He felt even more tired after his conversations with Jay and Gary. He was especially offended when Gary told him many people, even Albanians, were willing to work for less than eight dollars an hour. Sokol had done that a few years ago when he had worked as a company manager, and he was willing to do it again. He needed a steady job. As he was about to get in his car, his cell phone rang.

"Hello, Sokol," said Jacqueline's pleasant voice. "I'm calling to invite you to our wedding on September 16 in New York. Guess who else is coming? Besim, his wife, and his son as well as Marko and his fiancé. Besim even promised to sing a couple of old songs from Kosovo."

"Thank you so much for inviting me," said Sokol. "Imagine, a bunch of Albanians at an American wedding! How wonderful!"

Jacqueline's call had made Sokol's day.

PART II: SEPTEMBER 11, 2001 AROUND 7 AM

September in Boston has all four seasons. On summery days, people look for shade. On spring-like days, they take long walks in the evergreen parks. There are rainy fall days with gray skies and windy days reminiscent of winter, the longest and coldest season.

The weather on Tuesday, September 11, 2001 was magnificent. The sky seemed to kiss the Atlantic Ocean. The streets of Boston teemed with people walking to work, children holding their mothers' hands, teenagers going to school, tourists headed for Cape Cod, and travelers on their way to Logan Airport. In short, people went about their business unaware of what was about to happen.

At around 7 AM, Sokol and Jacqueline took their first coffee break. Jacqueline had just landed in Terminal B and was preparing to board the flight to Los Angeles. She wore her blue uniform. A small hat held some of her blond hair while the rest fell to her shoulders. The restaurant was crowded with passengers waiting for their flights. People talked and laughed loudly, but Sokol and Jacqueline managed to find a quiet area.

"Well, this is your last flight from this airport," said Sokol.

"It feels strange," said Jacqueline with a tremor in her voice. "I'm happy to be getting married, but I'm sad I won't be working here anymore. I'll miss my friends and colleagues: the pilots, the flight attendants, and the security personel, especially you, Sokol. Do you remember the day we met?"

"How could I forget?"

"Four years ago, I took my test to become a flight attendant, and you took yours to become a security employee. We were so happy, well, you not so much. You had to give up your career as a journalist when you came here and ended up doing something totally different."

"When I left Albania, I knew I had to start from scratch."

"I can't believe how much you've suffered. You told me about a music festival in the 1970's. You did everything you could to make it a success, and the dictator, Enver Hoxha, called it a show influenced by western music. He attacked everyone who loved the arts, and many innocent people, including you, were arrested. How awful! I suspect you have many sad memories you haven't shared with anyone."

Sokol smiled bitterly.

"The early 1990's saw the fall of Communism and the birth of democracy. After my release from prison, I started working for Albanian State Television again, but soon realized you can't remove Communism from people's minds. Some people made desperate attempts to revive it. Take 1997 for instance."

"If I'm not mistaken, many riots broke out during that time," said Jacqueline.

"That's right. People lost millions of dollars in savings because of the thieves who ran our country."

"And that's when you decided to leave Albania?"

"Yes. Armed militias roamed the streets, burned houses and office buildings, stole everything they could, and killed people for disobeying their orders."

"I remember seeing pictures on the news. I felt sorry for the innocent people who suffered, and I wanted them to come to Boston. I was fond of you. You worked hard even though you were not working in your profession."

"Thank you for your kind words."

"Last September, when Steve made his documentary for CNN

about Logan Airport, and you stood next to him, I realized I still had feelings for you."

A long line of passengers waited to go through the security checkpoint where Sokol worked. A few Arabs, among them Marvan and Muhammad, sat a little farther away, holding their bags and cups of tea.

"Brother Muhammad, do you remember what we talked about last May in this very terminal?" asked Marvan.

"How could I forget, Brother Marvan? As Osama bin Laden said in the Afghan forest, we will meet in Paradise. Abdul al Ramsey stood by his side."

"I remember Osama and Abdul very well," said Marvan, "though Abdul seemed quite distracted."

"He was very brave," said Muhammad. "I saw him fight in a village near Kandahar. Most of the residents were against the Taliban. We took them by surprise around midnight, but they were tough, fought back, and killed a lot of our men. We weren't so bad, either. Abdul was the bravest and killed anyone who got in his way, including women and children."

Marvan hugged Muhammad, waved to some other Arabs, and left. Muhammad kept an eye on him until he disappeared into the crowd. Their conversation still ringing in his ears, he turned to Abdul, who looked pale.

"Are you all right?"

"Why are you asking me that? I'm fine!"

"You look pale."

"I'm fine, never better."

"It's almost time to go through security. Hang

in there. You're a brave warrior. Everything will go smoothly. Just remember bin Laden's words and Allah will protect you."

. . .

Sokol and Jacqueline still sat in the restaurant. After a brief silence, Sokol said, "We will see each other again since I'm sure you'll fly from New York to Boston quite often."

"I'm going to request flights to Boston so I can see you. I also have quite a few cousins here."

Suddenly, Jacqueline felt the sadness she had experienced years ago after the loss of her parents within a short period of time. Sokol immediately changed the subject.

"A CNN reporter came to our airport, stole your heart, and took you to New York," he teased.

Jacqueline laughed.

"It didn't happen quite that way. We met on a flight to San Francisco and had a short conversation."

"Did you already love him then?"

Jacqueline blushed a little and laughed even harder.

"No. I was just surprised we had a well-known CNN reporter on board. When he came here to make his documentary, he recognized me and gave me a peck on the cheek."

"That way, he could give you a real kiss later," joked Sokol. "I'm sure you've kissed many times, but that kiss at the American Airlines dance was out of this world. Fatie and I were there, remember? They were playing Come Back in September."

Jacqueline smiled.

"I was dancing with Fatie. We were laughing because she had grown up under the Taliban in the mountains of Afghanistan and had never seen a modern dance. She didn't know how to dance. We were wearing bright colored clothes and were dancing in the middle of the floor until you and Steve joined us. You were so in love and couldn't take your eyes off each other. You didn't realize everybody had practically left you alone on the dance floor. You danced beautifully, like one person. The song played several times."

Jacqueline sang:

"Come back in September, the month we met,
So I can hold your hand
While we kiss under the tree,
And lay on the green grass.

Nothing but the dawn can separate us."

"You kissed each other," Sokol recalled. "We looked at you and shouted, Long live the lovers!"

Jacqueline covered her face with her hands and said, "No wonder you're a writer, the way you remember everything and describe everything so beautifully."

Her eyes shone, and she could not stop laughing.

"Steve is a good writer, too," she said. "He did a really good job writing the documentary about Albanians, and he nailed it with the title, The Eagle Above the Fort."

She paused for a few seconds then continued, "And the questions he asked, I get emotional every time I think about it. Or maybe I think so highly of him because I love him so much."

"To be sure, he's a competent journalist. Besim, Marta, and their son gave intelligent answers. The little one expressed his wish to go back to Kosovo and visit the villages where his parents were born and raised. You're right, Jacqueline. Steve's documentary was spot on. Well, your flight will probably be leaving soon."

"Yes, it will," said Jacqueline.

She and Sokol stood up at the same time. As she was leaving the restaurant, she saw the members of her crew.

"Thank goodness you remembered to join us," said Emma Jackson, another flight attendant. "Sokol was probably telling you stories about a new book. If you had been delayed any longer, we would have left you here."

"Then she would have flown to New York to see Steve," said Chris Frasier, a pilot who had been working for American Airlines for many years.

"We wouldn't have left without you," said Patrick Estrom, another pilot. "Especially not today, your last day with us. Your sense of humor makes you the heart of our crew."

"We plan to ask the passengers to raise a toast to the bride to be," said Chris.

"How wonderful!" cried Emma.

"I'm speechless," said Jacqueline. "I don't know what to say except thank you from the bottom of my heart!"

As Sokol was going back to work, he saw Jay Clement. He had only seen him a couple of times since their conversation in May, when he had suggested a few changes in protocol. Jay had not responded to Sokol's proposals and had not discussed them anymore. He nodded as he passed by.

"How strange," Sokol thought. "Didn't Jay tell his superiors about these problems? Or doesn't he think they're important?"

The passengers moved slowly toward the area where they would empty their pockets and put their belongings in small plastic bins to be scanned. With every beep, the workers checked the item in question. After an older man and his wife went through security without any difficulty, the man smiled and asked, "Do you remember me?"

Sokol looked at him and said, "I'm sorry. I see thousands of faces every day and it's hard to remember everyone."

"I'm George Bradley. Last spring, you told me to take off my belt. This time, I made sure to take it off and put everything that can trigger a beep in these bins."

At once, Sokol remembered him. He had been surprised when Sokol had asked him to take off his belt.

"I'm grateful you take precautions to ensure our safety," George continued.

"Thank you, sir. I wish more people would be as understanding as you are."

After the elderly couple left, Sokol saw a young man in his early twenties, dressed in a blue shirt, with short, black hair. It was Muhammad. He put his suitcase on the conveyor belt and took some coins as well as a small knife out of his pocket. He smiled as he waited for his luggage. Sokol measured the knife. Its size conformed to FAA regulations, but it was sharper than other knives he had seen.

"Is something wrong?" asked Muhammad.

From his accent, Sokol knew the man came from an Arab country.

"No, Sir, everything is fine. You may proceed. However, I noticed your little knife is quite sharp."

"I like to fish," said Muhammad. "I use the knife to clean and cook the fish I catch."

"That's what I thought," said Jacqueline, who stood behind Sokol. Sokol was still suspicious. He saw Gary sitting in the restaurant and considered asking his opinion about the knife, which looked even sharper in the light, but he figured he would ignore him. Therefore, he said, "You're good to go, Sir."

After the man left, Jacqueline went through security, and Sokol scanned her bag.

"I'll see you at our wedding," said Jacqueline. "We decided to go to Albania for our honeymoon. We're going to Saranda because Besim described it so beautifully."

She said good-bye to Sokol and Fatie.

"I'll see you soon," she said.

"You bet," said Fatie, "but before you go, we have something for you."

The other passengers had overheard Jacqueline's and Fatie's conversation and wanted to find out what was going on. Suddenly, they heard a beautiful song:

"We wish you and your beloved Steve
A happy marriage.
May you always be blessed!"

Jacqueline stood there, stunned while other people looked at her, among them, two security employees, a thin, young girl from Indonesia, who worked in maintenance, a man in his forties from Bangladesh who worked in a coffee shop, and a few other American Airlines employees, who worked in Terminal B. All at once, a young girl from Morocco pulled a bouquet of roses and a box from behind her back.

"This was Sokol and Fatie's idea," she said, hugging Jacqueline and handing her the flowers and the box. Then everyone else hugged her and wished her all the best. She kept looking at Sokol and Fatie, who couldn't leave their stations.

"Okay, let's go before she changes her mind," said Emma.

"She'll be a hard act to follow," said Chris.

"We're gonna miss you," said Emma.

"Me, too," said a young girl named Greta Vozinsky. "This is my first flight."

"You never forget your first flight," said Jacqueline. "It's like your first love. It lives in your heart forever."

Jacqueline looked at the crew who had treated her kindly and thought about the many flights they had worked together. It made her sad to realize this was her last flight with them.

After she boarded the plane, she called Steve.

"Hi, Honey. We'll be leaving for Los Angeles in about an hour. You'll never guess what happened."

"What?"

Jacqueline related the morning's events.

"If they love you that much, imagine how I feel. I'm crazy about you," said Steve. "Come and see me as soon as you can. I'm afraid I'll die if I don't see you!"

"I feel the same way," said Jacqueline. "Just two more days and we'll be together for good."

In the course of about half an hour, while Sokol covered for a worker on break, hundreds of passengers, most bound for Los Angeles, went through security. As she inspected the luggage, Fatie noticed several glass bottles, most of which contained alcoholic beverages, as well as a large number of perfume bottles. If she saw small metallic objects, such as a pocket knife, she stopped the belt to make sure everything was in order. Sokol measured the knives to ensure their length conformed to the size allowed by the FAA. If passengers carried knives which were longer than the maximum size allowed, he asked them to fill out a form and leave their knives with the security personel.

A young man, Abdul, carried a small knife with which Sokol almost cut himself.

"Wow! That's a sharp knife!" he said.

Abdul looked like an Arab who had just gone through security with a similar knife. But while the other man had smiled, Abdul looked more serious, even sick. He said he hadn't realized how sharp his knife was.

"I just bought it," he said. "Its handmade handle caught my eye. Am I not allowed to take it with me? It only cost five dollars."

"You're allowed to have it since it's a small knife," said Sokol.

With that, Abdul went through security. Gary motioned to Sokol to meet him in the restaurant, where a small farewell ceremony had been organized for Jacqueline. While Sokol waited for the worker who would cover for him during his meeting, he wondered why Gary wanted to see him. He had checked every object carefully. Had there been a problem with the last passenger?

Sokol knew Gary wasn't in a good mood the moment he saw him.

"What was the deal with the passenger who carried a pocket knife?"

Sokol, who sensed a storm brewing, explained

what had happened.

"Why did you stress the knife's sharpness? Don't you realize you could have caused a misunderstanding? You've been at this job for four years. You're a journalist, a writer, with a lot of experience. Didn't it occur to you the passenger could file a complaint with the FAA, with Jay Clement himself? Why do you make such remarks if you know the object in question is allowed on board?"

Sokol felt a pang of guilt.

"I was struck by the sharpness of the blade. It could cut a person's throat. I apologize."

"Very well. Just don't lecture me like you lectured Jay about what should and shouldn't be allowed on the plane. It's none of your business. I told you once and I'll say it again. Just follow the rules. I'm planning a staff meeting in regard to this problem. Now go back to work."

He left without giving Sokol a chance to say more.

American Airlines Flight 11 would soon depart from Boston for Los Angeles. Muhammad and Abdul, looking tired and concerned, sat close together. The other three Arabs seemed happy, like the other passengers, most of whom looked forward to seeing their loved ones. George and Amanda noticed how happy the three young men looked. No one knew about their evil intentions. Their smiles masked imminent death.

Muhammad and Abdul whispered to each other. Muhammad said to Abdul in Arabic, "Calm down. We made it through security with our knives and bottles. I hope Marvan and his friends made it. Keep smiling. Don't look so distressed. Otherwise, you'll draw attention to yourself."

"I got scared when the security worker pointed out the sharpness of my knife," said Abdul.

"I felt the same way," said Muhammad, "but thank Allah, one of the flight attendants, the blond one, walked by while the security worker was talking to me."

"I saw her. I heard her say you could only cut a fish with that knife. It's funny they didn't ask you anything, Vail."

"I was surprised, too," said

Vail. "It was the same security worker who was here last year when I went through this same checkpoint. He just measured my knife. He didn't say a word."

"That's strange," said Muhammad.

"I saw someone motion to him to meet him in the restaurant," said Rashid, Muhammad's brother.

"I saw that, too," said Satem.

"Who could that have been?" asked Abdul.

"Probably the supervisor," said Satem.

"That explains everything," said Muhammad.

"I would have done the same thing. He was just doing his job," said Vail.

"I know the FAA rules. Our knives were allowed on board. That worker had no right to ask questions."

"You're right," said Satem. "He was trying to provoke us."

"Exactly," said Muhammad. "His job was to measure the knives and if they were longer than the maximum size allowed, he could have said something. Otherwise, he should have kept his mouth shut."

"We can file a complaint against him, right?" said Rashid.

"Of course," said Muhammad. "But there's no need. We made it through security, and that's all that matters. I don't know what's the matter with Abdul, though."

"Indeed, my brother, you look pale," said Satem.

"I got scared and nervous at the checkpoint. What if they had taken away our knives? I didn't say anything because I didn't want to worry you, but it could have happened. Then we wouldn't have been able to perform our sacred duty."

"Don't say any more. We made it through security with our knives and perfume bottles filled with tear gas. Now we can keep our promise to Allah," said Muhammad, looking at his cohorts.

"No one can stop us!" said Satem.

"No one!" affirmed the rest in unison.

"Then let us smile even more," said Muhammad. "Today is our holy day. Today we are going to Allah's kingdom. We will be heroes!"

The whole group felt a little uneasy. They were about to embark on the greatest mission of their lives and were going to their eternal home. Recently, on a cold and windy night, Muhammad, Marvan, and the others talked about this day on the third floor of an old building in Hamburg. Unfortunately, no one overheard their conversation then or now.

"I don't know why," Muhammad thought, "but that blond flight attendant who said my knife didn't pose a threat reminded me of Sharon, a blond American I met in Hamburg. She always smiled like her. I, an Egyptian from Cairo, who had just moved to Hamburg, could have loved her if she hadn't been an American. But I hated her the way I hated all Americans. She never approached me or talked to me. I can't say she hated me, but I couldn't stand it that she didn't make the first move. I wanted her to fall in love with me so I could put her down. I wanted her to

adore me and be submissive to this Egyptian, an architect who studied in the land of pyramids, designed and built by my ancestors hundreds of years ago when America was home to the Indians as the Europeans called them when Columbus discovered their country. The Europeans didn't civilize them. They took their land by force. Soon everybody was fighting over the land, women were raped, men were hunted down, and many became slaves. Later, the whites brought blacks from Africa. That's how America became a superpower. My friends and I promised bin Laden, the Almighty Creator Allah, and His son, Muhammad, whose name I bear with pride, that we would dispel the myth that Americans live in peace and harmony, regardless of religion, that the American people would suffer and die. Great Allah, you are about to meet ten of your most faithful followers who now sit in four planes, ready to embark on their sacred mission.

"Satem al Sukami is a law student at the Royal University of Rabat in Saudi Arabia. Abdul al Ramzi is married with a two-year-old son he has never met. Before our departure, he acted strange. Please, Allah, he said, May I be wrong! Vail al Shehri, a teacher, and his brother, Rashid, a construction worker, are from Qatar and are bound and determined to fulfill their obligation. Marvan al Shehin and others faithful to Allah are in the other plane."

Muhammad rose from his seat and looked at the many passengers who were preparing to board, among them Marvan and the other Arabs. That same morning, other brothers with the same mission departed on flights from New Jersey and Washington. Marvan's and Muhammad's eyes met. Marvan smiled and nodded. Muhammad took a deep breath and said,

"Everything is going as planned. Now, talk and laugh. We don't want to look suspicious."

"Ah, youth," George whispered.

"Who knows what kind of jokes they're telling," said his wife.

"They're Arabs. They're probably reciting parts of A Thousand and One Nights," said George. “They're wonderful stories."

No one could have imagined the horrible tragedy these young men would set in motion.

As soon as the passengers had been told to board their flight from Boston to Los Angeles, Muhammad took his phone out of his pocket, dialed a number, and said sotta voce, "Brother Jaser, we are about to board our plane. Marvan and the other brothers are about to board the other plane. In the name of Allah, do your job. We will meet again soon in you know where."

Jaser sat in his office in one of the Twin Towers, his face aglow.

"Marvan al Shehin just called me," he said. "Everything is going according to plan."

Everyone rejoiced when Muhammad told them what Jaser had said.

"Marvan is brave and loyal," said Satem.

"He is one of a kind," said Vail.

"That's why he's one of bin Laden's favorites," said Rashid.

"If I was on my death bed, he'd only have to look at me once, and I'd burn myself alive for him," said Muhammad. "I'm ready to die with you. I'm glad we're eliminating the infidels."

"Me, too," said Satem. "I can't wait to cut their throats and capture them. No matter what happens, the thought of bin Laden will give us the strength to accomplish our sacred mission, right, my brothers?"

Everyone nodded in agreement.

"As you know, I love Marvan with all my heart because he was the mastermind behind the 1998 attack on the American Embassy in Nairobi which killed 223 people and wounded hundreds more. He managed to plant the bombs without anyone noticing him. At the time, he was a freshman in college. His campus was near my house in Hamburg. He used to tell me stories about his work with bin Laden. If you, who met him in person, envy him, what about the rest of us who never even saw him? It's true, Abdul and I met him one night, but we haven't worked closely with him yet."

After their hushed conversation, the Arabs clutched their knives in their pockets as if they feared someone would take them away. Before they boarded the plane, they looked out the airport window one last time. The planes seemed to be sleeping in the sun. However, the beautiful sight did not impress them. 250 miles from Logan International Airport, Besim and Marko stopped to see Said in his office on the 25th floor of Tower 1 before continuing to the 107th floor to clean the windows.

"It's a beautiful, sunny day without much wind," said Besim.

"It is," said Said.

"I wish we had days like this in the winter," said Besim.

"It's a different world up there," said Said. "That's what makes your job so difficult. You were right when you said in Steve Ferguson's documentary you are like eagles that fly high above the mountains to provide for their young regardless of the weather.

"That's true," said Besim.

"I really liked the documentary," said Said.

"Steve did a great job," said Besim.

"With a fiancé as pretty as Jacqueline, who wouldn't be inspired to do the best job possible," said Marko.

"Speaking of Jacqueline, Sokol told me this is her last flight

from Boston," said Besim. "She'll be moving here right before the wedding. I hope you and Serena can come."

"I hope so, too. Serena is due in two weeks. She's having a girl."

"Really!" said Besim. "Albanians prefer their firstborn to be boys. Years ago, we needed boys in Albania to fight the Turks and

boys in Kosovo to fight the Serbs. But don't be sorry you're having a girl. We need girls, too."

"How would you feel if Marta gave birth to a girl instead of a boy?" asked Said with a smirk.

Besim remained silent for a few moments, then said, "I'd teach her, like Trim, to use a gun. During the wars, girls fought with us when necessary."

Besim looked at his watch and said, "It's time for us eagles to go to our nest." He and Said laughed.

"Stay safe up there,," said Said.

Just then, Said's phone rang. After he hung up, he said to Marko, "There's an electrical problem in the other tower. Unfortunately, your box is not working, but they are trying to fix it. In the meantime, go and help Besim."

"I will, especially since he won't be working here much longer. He takes good care of me. He is afraid of me getting hurt."

Besim hugged Marko. As they left Said's office, they ran into Jaser, on his way to the office with a stack of papers.

"Besim looks so young," said Jaser.

"He sure does," said Said. "I'm sure he won't sit around after he retires. Maybe he'll get a job as a teacher when he goes back to Kosovo. He used to be a teacher."

"He's still planning to go back to Kosovo?"

"He can't wait to go back. He's counting the days."

"Days? He should be counting the hours," thought Jaser.

While Said and Jaser were talking, Serena came in, as beautiful as ever, even though she had gained weight during her pregnancy. She greeted Jaser as he placed the papers he was carrying on the desk.

"Sweetheart," she said to Said, "I called you several times on your cell phone, but you didn't answer."

"I'm so sorry," said Said. "I accidentally shut my phone off."

He stood up.

"You should have called me at the office."

"I did," said Serena, "but the line was busy."

"I was sending a fax. What happened? Why are you here?"

"The doctor called. He won't be able to see us at noon so he asked if we could come earlier."

Jaser had all he could do to keep from screaming.

"Can't we go later?" asked Said. "Jaser and I wanted to finish some work we've been putting off for a while."

"Why don't you drop me off and I'll call you when I'm done."

"I'm sure our work will take us a couple of hours."

Said took the papers Jaser had left on the desk and told Jaser he would be back as soon as possible. Jaser smiled and nodded, but when he saw Said and Serena holding hands, his smile changed to a frown.

Jaser said to himself in Arabic, "I just received word from Boston that my friends, led by Muhammad Ata, have just departed from Logan Airport and will soon come here to keep the promise they made to Almighty Allah. Therefore, don't take too long, Said! We'll talk later."

As he said these words, his eyes widened and sparkled with satisfaction, His face looked devilish as he said, "A curse on your American wife, an infidel!" He pounded the desk with his fist.

Besim, Marko, and Rrok entered the elevator and went up to the 107th floor.

"When Steve came here last May to

work on his documentary, he and Jacqueline, went all the way up to the 107th floor," said Rrok. "Hey, Marko, you never brought your fiancé so we could meet her. I met her last night, and let me tell you, she's very pretty. I happened to see her with Marko as they got on the subway to go to the Bronx. They were holding hands. Marko didn't even see me. That's how in love he is."

"Well, why didn't you say something?" asked Marko.

"I didn't want to interrupt your moment of love."

"Is she that pretty?" asked Besim.

"Of course," said Rrok. "A handsome, young man like Marko would only choose the prettiest girl."

Marko shook his head and said, "Don't mind him, Besim. He is exaggerating. My Maria is beautiful, but more important, she is a beautiful person inside.

"We will see you this Sunday at Steve and Jacqueline's wedding," said Besim.

"Do I have to bring her, too?" Marko teased.

"Weren't you listening when Steve and Jacqueline invited both of you to the wedding?" asked Besim.

"Of course," said Marko.

"There you go," said Besim. "There'll be Said and Serena, Sokol, you and Maria, Marta, Trim, and I. You can announce your engagement at the wedding. Are you coming, Rrok?"

"I wasn't invited," he said.

"Come on, man, Steve and Jacqueline would be thrilled to see you. They felt bad when you told them you're single. Why don't you come? We'll have a good time. We can sing a few songs from Kosovo together, like *Moj e bukura More*, which Steve and Jacqueline loved."

"Amazing!" said Rrok. "An American wedding and an Arberesh engagement."

At 7:59 AM, American Airlines Flight 11 prepared to depart for Los Angeles from Logan International Airport. Pilots Chris Frasier and Patrick Estrom started the airplane's engines. Jacqueline and Emma helped passengers to their seats, among them, Muhammad, Abdul, and Satem, who flew in first class. Vail and Rashid flew in economy. Muhammad took his phone out of his pocket and dialed a number.

"Marvan," he said. "We are about to leave. "What's going on?"

"We're boarding now."

"Have a good flight, Brother Marvan."

"You, too, Muhammad."

A few minutes later, the plane roared like a large animal as it ascended into the blue sky. The Arabs pretended to sleep. Jacqueline looked out the window. The tall buildings disappeared as the plane flew into the fluffy clouds. She thought of Steve, whom she had met on this very plane. She would never forget his interview with her for his documentary, *A Day at Logan International Airport, Boston 2000.* While deep in thought, Emma approached her.

"Every time we take off, I think of Steve's first question when he interviewed me: "Why do you like your job?" said Jacqueline.

"I remember him asking you that," said Emma. "You gave a splendid answer and made some comparisons I don't remember right now, something about fishermen if I'm not mistaken."

"That's right. I said fishermen love the sea, the waves, and the wind that pushes their boats, sometimes slowly, sometimes furiously."

"Oh yes, now I remember. You also said the plane is your boat, and you sail the skies, which are sometimes calm and other times stormy like the sea. I also remember Steve asking you if you were ever scared. You said accidents don't just happen in the sky, but also on the ground when people walk or drive. I feel free as a bird up here. I feel like I'm flying."

Jacqueline and Emma didn't realize Greta had joined them and had overheard their conversation.

"I feel the same way," she said.

"And you will after a hundred flights," said Jacqueline.

"Even when you go home, you'll be ready to go back to work," said Emma.

"My mom will celebrate her 50th birthday in two days," said Greta.

"Wow! Half a century!" said Jacqueline. "That's pretty special."

Chris and Patrick felt like birds, too, and loved their job.

"So, Chris, you're leaving us, too," said Patrick.

"It would have been easier if they'd said I wasn't able to fly," said Chris with a frown.

"In any case, you'll still be at the controls."

"Yes, but just as an instructor. I'll only work a few hours a week, teaching other people to fly instead of thousands of hours flying all over the world."

"Well, someone has to teach people how to fly. Imagine if experienced pilots like you refused to do that?"

Chris remained silent.

"Would you become an instructor at the Aviation Academy if you had the chance?" asked Chris.

"In a heartbeat," said Patrick. "But I don't have your experience. Besides, you have a good reputation. Everyone at Logan knows who you are."

Chris recalled an incident from several years ago. During a landing, one of the engines stalled, and the plane almost crashed into some nearby houses. Needless to say, the terrified passengers panicked. However, Chris managed to land and avoid a collision, thereby saving the lives of about three hundred passengers.

Patrick interrupted Chris's thoughts when he said, "One day, someone may come up to you and say, Do you remember me, Mr. Frasier? I was one of your students at the Academy. Wouldn't you feel proud?"

Chris nodded. Still, he thought about the fact that today was his last flight. He had been a pilot for twenty years.

After the passengers watched a short safety video, Emma put a hand on Jacqueline's shoulder and said, "Ladies and gentlemen, today's flight is very special. It's our friend, Jacqueline's, last flight from Boston. She is getting married and will live in New York. Later, I will ask you to raise a toast to her and her future husband, a well known CNN reporter named Steve Ferguson."

The passengers applauded.

"Congratulations," said George. "I've never heard news like that on a plane."

"I haven't, either," said his wife, Amanda.

She stood up, gave Jacqueline a kiss, and embraced her.

"This deserves a special toast," said a tall, skinny man. "I am attending an international conference on lung cancer in Los Angeles, and I brought a couple of bottles of wine to celebrate with the other doctors and scientists, but I think we should open one of the bottles right now."

"I agree," said George. "My wife and I also brought a couple of bottles of wine. Our daughter just graduated with a degree in computer science, and we're going to celebrate that."

"Please, let's just use our wine," said Jacqueline.

"She's right," said Amanda. "Do you want us to land drunk in LA?"

"I'm not the only one celebrating," said George. "Other passengers want to celebrate, too. What about you gentlemen?"

He looked at Muhammad, Abdul, and Satem, but they just stared at each other.

"George, do you remember that man?" asked Amanda, pointing to Muhammad.

Suddenly, Muhammad felt uneasy for he thought Amanda might have overheard his conversation with the security worker about the pocket knife.

"I remember you," said George to the three young men. "You and your friends were talking, laughing, and having fun. Why not keep it going?"

Muhammad and his friends were very nervous and could hardly breathe as they thought about what was going to happen any minute. And now this.

Muhammad, facing the old couple, said, "Drinking is against our religion, but I think we should raise a toast. As a matter of fact, we have a bottle of wine which was supposed to be a gift for our friend in LA."

Muhammad took a wine bottle out of his bag.

"We have enough refreshments for everyone," said Jacqueline.

Then, she stared at Muhammad and wondered if they had met at security.

"Yes, I remember, you were delayed for a while because you had a small knife."

"Why did she have to say that?" thought Muhammad. "Will she scream for help because I have a knife and am attacking her?"

He clutched the knife in his pocket as he looked at Jacqueline. She continued to look at him and smiled.

"My friend was wrong," she said. "I assured him you can't cut anything with that kind of knife except, maybe a small bird."

"I appreciate you telling him that, Ma'am. For a second there, I thought I would miss my flight. He insisted the knife was sharp."

"He did indeed, but you can't blame him. Times have changed.

He was just doing his job."

"I wish he was on the plane with us," thought Muhammad. "Then, he'd see what I'm capable of."

Jacqueline went to economy, where Emma and the other flight attendants were. Suddenly, everyone started clapping,

and Emma shouted, "Here comes the bride!"

Passengers congratulated Jacqueline.

"All the best to you and Steve!" said Emma.

Jacqueline winked at her. She couldn't wait to call Steve and tell him everything.

Meanwhile, the man in first class was trying to open a wine bottle George had given him.

"George, you heard the flight attendant. There's enough wine for everyone," said Amanda.

"She's right. Let's wait for the flight attendants to serve us wine," said the man, putting the bottle back in his bag.

George did the same even though he couldn't wait to have a glass.

"Hopefully, you'll find a cure for that awful disease, which kills hundreds and thousands of people," said Amanda.

"That would be nice," said the doctor, "but people need to quit smoking, too." "That's right," said George. "I'm glad I did."

"You quit smoking, but you drink wine," said Amanda.

"So what? Did anyone die from drinking wine?" said George, looking at the doctor.

"No," he said. "As a matter of fact, people have come back to life after drinking wine."

Everyone laughed. Muhammad and his cohorts, though nervous, laughed, too.

"Laugh as much as you can. You are cursed infidels. Soon you'll be crying for help," Muhammad thought.

First class became quiet. People read, slept, watched a movie, or sipped drinks. Muhammad noticed Abdul's unease. He told him to stay calm and think about how fortunate they were to have met bin Laden. Abdul forced a smile. Although he was pretty sure none of the other passengers spoke or understood Arabic, he made certain no one was looking at him.

"You and Vail should rejoice with the rest of our brothers for soon we will be in heaven, right, Satem?"

Satem, who sat to the right of Muhammad, flashed his eyes at him.

"I'm ready to keep the promise we gave to Allah," said Satem.

He thought of an old professor at the Royal University of Rabat who used to say softly, "A judge has one mother, one father and one family who are holy, but justice and Allah's teachings are even holier. Allah teaches us to fight the infidels who will never see heaven's gates."

"Heaven?" thought Abdul. "If my wife, whom I haven't seen in over two years, and my two-year-old son, whom I've never met, don't go to heaven, what's the point? I didn't consider that when I met bin Laden, the world's most faithful Muslim, the leader of al Qaeda, who is fighting the infidels. He called us faithful, too, when we trained in the secret military camps in Afghanistan. One cold night, he called for us. No one, not even our group, could know his whereabouts. Therefore, our escort blindfolded us. We walked through the mountains and entered a creepy-looking cave, lit by torches. We met bin Laden himself. He was dressed in white, and his long beard had some gray hairs. He looked like a noble reincarnation of Muhammad. We stood before the man who had given up his career as an engineer to fight the Mujahideen. When he fought the Russians, he even gave up his wealth to support Islam's war against Christianity. We kneeled before him and kissed his hand with respect. His beautiful voice commanded us to fight soldiers and civilians throughout the world. We had already killed many civilians in Nairobi, Dar el Salam, and other places.

"That night, we learned about our next mission, not from bin Laden, but from a man to his right with a long beard, Khalid Sheikh

Muhammad, bin Laden's best friend, whose look seemed to penetrate our souls, and who seemed to want to hear our heartbeats. He told us we would not be killing Americans, Europeans, or other peoples with weapons, as we had done previously. We weren't going to kill them on streets, trains, or buses. We weren't going to kill nonbelieving Muslims like the ones I killed in Kandahar who fought the Taliban. We weren't going to set off bombs or hijack planes and hold passengers hostage in exchange for the release of imprisoned Muslim brothers. With each word, Khalid's voice grew more intense like the wind before a storm. You are going to sacrifice your lives, said bin Laden. You and other passengers will die together. You will learn to fly planes and will crash them into the two tallest buildings in New York, the pride of America. It'll be glorious. The buildings will burn and collapse, burying many people. This is your mission. Do you accept it? Are you, my brothers, willing to sacrifice your lives?

"Bin Laden's and Khalid Sheikh Muhammad's eyes bore into us. I thought about the Imam who preached about the Koran in the village where I was born and raised. He used to say those who were faithful to Allah and did good in this world would be rewarded in the next. Before bin Laden had finished speaking, we knelt before him and kissed his feet. How could we not accept this mission, great bin Laden? said Marvan. This is a faithful Muslim's greatest privilege, said Muhammad. Very well, said bin Laden as he patted our heads.

"That was two years ago. Now we're here, about to embark on our holy mission. Will we really go to heaven?"

Vail and Rashid looked like bearded twins. They waited impatiently for Muhammad's call to tell them their mission had begun. They recalled their days in the cold and mud, learning how to survive in the camps near the Pakistani border, and they remembered bin Laden's preaching:

"On Judgment Day, you will be held accountable for your deeds in this life. The greater your deeds, the greater your reward will be. The Almighty Allah will reward this, your greatest deed.

Rashid thought about his brother, Nuredin, a member of al Qaeda, who fought in Afghanistan, and had sacrificed everything to join the Army. Because he was skinny, he found the intense training and fasting difficult. Bin Laden used to tell the soldiers how, from the beginning of time, western nations fought Islamic nations because they wanted to liberate Jerusalem from the Turks. He related an incident which occurred over a thousand years earlier, 1907 years to be exact. One morning in a small Arabian village, the men worked in the fields while most of the women, children, and elderly slept. Suddenly, people ran from their homes, screaming, as soldiers dressed in white overalls with large, black crosses on their chests raided the village, killed anyone who got in their way, and raped women and young girls in front of the children. They killed every single person in the village, except for an old man, who escaped to a nearby village and told everyone what had happened. The soldiers had come from Europe, supposedly to free Jerusalem from the Turks, but why did they have to kill and rape innocent people along the way, and why did they undertake so many crusades over a period of 200 years?

When Rashid heard this story, he remembered reading in school about what the Arabs taught the Europeans. The Arabs had occupied Sicily and Spain but had not killed or raped innocent people. The Koran didn't teach that. They built roads, schools, parks, and other structures. They also taught the Europeans different methods of irrigation and brought them various plants, including rice. But most important, the Arabs let the Europeans practice their religion, Christianity.

"And how did they repay us?" Rashid thought. "By destroying everything we did, killing, and raping. That's why we Muslims hate Christians."

Rashid and his brother overheard two men in front of them talking about Islamic fundamentalism and terrorism. Rashid jumped to his feet and pretended to adjust his bag. He saw a copy of "The Boston Globe" and the headline, "Another victory for the American forces against bin Laden's terrorists in Afghanistan." A picture below the title showed American soldiers with Taliban prisoners. Rashid sat down again.

"Who knows when these Islamic fundamentalists will be captured or killed?" said one of the men. "Just when we think we're making progress, other terrorists take revenge by blowing themselves up, taking innocent people with them."

"It's all bin Laden's fault. He's the one nourishing the hatred by telling his followers stories about the Crusades. He uses an event that happened centuries ago to justify his acts of evil. He and his followers are proud to be called fundamentalists. Moderate Muslims do not condone their actions. Bin Laden says Allah's Law must rule from the deserts of Saudi Arabia to college campuses in America."

"That's absurd!" laughed the other man.

"There's more," said the first. "According to bin Laden, people should not be classified according to race or nationality, but according to their religion. He doesn't believe in states or nations. Everybody should belong to a single Islamic state, like the ancient Arabian Khalifate."

"I remember an Islamic fundamentalist, captured by American forces in Kenya, who said the Islamic fundamentalists consider Jihad, the holy war against the satanic West, the only solution with their main target the United States. That's why new al Qaeda units emerge every day with members from different countries: Saudi Arabia, Pakistan, Chechnya. Even European Christians have joined the so-called Jihad. The Muslims have an advantage."

"What do you mean?" asked his friend, surprised.

"To them, death is a temporary state until they go to heaven. The other day, I read an article in the paper about bin Laden's right hand man, Khalid Sheikh Muhammad, who said there will be many more large scale attacks in the future, and a lot of Christians will die."

"You must give them credit, though. They are brave."

"Imagine carrying a bomb around your waist just so you can kill yourself and other people! That's not bravery, that's sheer stupidity and a crime!"

Rashid was about to speak, but Vail stopped him. The two men talked for a few more minutes. Then, one of them asked his friend if he wanted a cigarette.

"No," he said. "I had one just before we boarded. I smoke one every hour or so."

"It's not the end of the world if you smoke two cigarettes an hour. Besides, after today, smoking won't be allowed on planes anymore."

"I heard that," he said, then went to join his friend. The two Arab brothers remained in their seats.

"Did you hear those stupid Americans?" asked Vail.

"I certainly did," said Rashid. "Thank God you grabbed my arm. I almost grabbed them by their throats."

"That would have been the dumbest thing ever," said Vail. "Remember what Sheikh said, we have to be cautious. You almost lost it. Stay cool. We're just moments away from our sacred mission."

"Are you scared?" asked Rashid. "You're shaking, just when Muhammad is about to give us the go ahead."

"I'm not scared," said Vail. "I would have slit the throats of those Americans, too. Remember when we caught that American couple a few years ago in that village in Lebanon? The wife was several months pregnant. I couldn't wait until we contacted the American Embassy in Beirut to exchange prisoners. I killed that couple right away. Then, I felt bad because I thought of our mother, left alone."

"I told you not to think about Mom, especially now," said Rashid.

"I'll forget her, but she won't forget me," said Vail. "Every time Marvan, Muhammad, Abdul, and I went to the camps, she would ask us where we were going and why we stayed away so long. Then, she prayed for our safe return to Qatar, embraced us, and sniffed us."

"You know, Vail, you and Abdul should not have come on this mission. You're not cut out for it. Even though you're more educated than me, you rush into things."

"I can't help it. How will our mother cope with the news that both her sons are dead, that they did such a horrible thing? Her whole world will be shattered. Yesterday, Abdul told me he is leaving behind his only son. He never even met him."

Rashid could hardly keep from screaming.

"At least one of us should have stayed home."

"I wish I could kill you myself, you coward! I hope you rot in hell!" Rashid almost screamed.

Vail didn't even hear his brother's curse. He imagined his mother, waiting for her two boys, whom she raised with a lot of tears and sacrifice, since her husband's death. Every time they came home, she begged them to get married and have children so she could take care of them with the same love she had shown her boys. When Rashid worked as a teacher, he sometimes held classes at home. The laughter of children had not filled the house for many years. Every time Rashid and Vail left, their mother prayed for their safe return. She even prayed for them when they slept and smelled their clothes if she couldn't embrace them.

One night, not long after their return from Afghanistan, Rashid and Vail's mother approached their beds while they slept.

"What's wrong, Mom?" asked Vail.

"Nothing, Son," she said. "I couldn't sleep and came to cover you up. Your blanket had fallen on the floor."

But Vail knew his mother was watching him and Rashid and praying for them.

"I'm not a coward," said Vail, "but I should have told Marvan you wouldn't be part of this. At least you would have been alive and would have stayed home with Mom."

"If only I had known you felt that way, I would have asked Marvan if you could stay home with our mother, but it's too late."

Rashid squeezed Vail's hand so hard he almost screamed in pain. He was hallucinating and said, "For the love of Allah, go away, you ugly thoughts, and stop tormenting me. These Americans are the great grandchildren of the people who killed our ancestors and mocked our religion. They still do, and the time has come for you, Muhammad, and the rest of us to fulfill our obligation to bin Laden and Khalid Sheikh Muhammad in the name of Allah the Almighty."

"That's the spirit," said Rashid, putting his hand on his brother's shoulder.

Abdul thought the same thing, not because he wanted to but because Muhammad told him such thoughts would strengthen their resolve to take revenge on western infidels. Abdul recalled his training in the forests of Kandahar.

"Both the British and Americans supported the right of nonpracticing Jews to build on Palestinian land," Marvan had said. "In 1967, the Americans began their occupation of Arab teritory."

Abdul had listened along with everyone else but had had second thoughts after meeting Muhammad, other Taliban fighters, and ordinary people. He and many other Muslims, did not approve of the fundamentalists' so-called war against the Christians. He avoided buses and coffee shops for fear people might accuse him of being a terrorist and kill him.

Indeed, Abdul had become a murderer. Once, he had encountered a woman, her two children, and their grandfather.

"My son killed Taliban fighters. Kill me, but let this woman and her children go!" the old man pleaded.

Abdul killed them all. Still, he was suspicious of Marvan, other Taliban fighters, and bin Laden even though they were as ruthless as he was.

Satem recalled a night when, as he was about to go to sleep in a tent in Lebanon, Marvan gave a speech to the soldiers.

"We are proud to be called fundamentalists," he said. "Allah's law must extend from the Saudi Arabian desert to American university campuses. People should not be separated by race or nationality but by religion. We must form a single Islamic state like the ancient Khalifate."

Satem also thought of bin Laden, who would often say, "The only way to achieve our goal is with a Jihad against the evil West. The mission, for which we are preparing, is part of our war. Soon we will attack America, Satan's home. We will win the war. We are not afraid of death."

Satem's and Muhammad's blood boiled. Muhammad thought of Sheikh Khalid who had said, "When you are about to embark on one of our missions against the western non-believers, think of Jihad. Our brothers who have killed many people will be rewarded with eternal life."

Suddenly, Abdul started coughing and could hardly breathe. Satem, afraid the Americans might become suspicious, whispered, "Brother Abdul, despite Muhammad's encouragement, you're still having second thoughts. One of my professors in law school said we had the right to condemn anyone who didn't accept our religion, and we have people like that on this flight, do you understand?"

Satem looked at Abdul for a couple of minutes.

Greta, Jacqueline, and Emma, pushed carts with drinks.

"We are coming around with champagne and wine for a toast to Jacqueline," said Emma.

As she filled the glasses, one could see a small cross hanging from her neck. It seemed to Vail that Emma's cross grew larger and her hair grew longer. Only her cold, savage eyes remained visible. Vail thought a man stood in front of him, not holding a wine bottle, but a sword. Emma looked like one of the crusaders, described by Nuredin and Vail's teacher, who plundered villages.

At that moment, Vail's phone rang, Muhammad's signal to attack. The men sprang to their feet and accosted Emma. Muhammad and Satem clutched small perfume bottles with poison gas. None of the other passengers knew what was happening.

"May I help you?" asked Emma, aware of two passengers standing in front of her.

Abdul grabbed her by the shoulders while Satem sprayed her in the face. She fainted in shock. After Satem disposed of the bottle, he pulled his knife out of his pocket. The other passengers, stunned by the scene, became speechless.

Satem told Emma if she moved, he would cut her throat. To prove he meant what he said, he closed her mouth and stabbed her in the throat. She flinched as she bled out, tried to speak, but couldn't.

Meanwhile, Muhammad knocked on the cockpit door and shouted, "Help! One of the flight attendants is sick!"

Chris motioned to Patrick to open the door, and as soon as he did, Muhammad beat him with a bottle until he bled and fell to the floor. Then, he cut his throat. The terrified passengers watched their pilot bleed to death.

"Do you want to end up like him?" Muhammad threatened, wiping the blood from his face and hands.

Chris could not see because the cockpit door was ajar, but he knew from the commotion something was wrong so he left the controls to investigate the situation. When he came out of the cockpit, Muhammad sprayed him and attempted to stab him.

Blinded by the spray, he tried to grab Muhammad's hand.

Muhammad stabbed him several more times in the throat. Chris tried to defend himself, but Muhammad stabbed him again. As Chris attempted to remove the knife from his throat, Muhammad picked up the metal bottle he had thrown on the floor and hit him several times on the head.

Meanwhile, Satem entered the cockpit and took control of the plane. Vail and Rashid stabbed Emma in the throat. Jacqueline and two other flight attendants tried to interveen but backed away after Rashid threatened to cut their throats.

"Nobody move!" Vail shouted. "If you keep quiet, nothing bad will happen."

Muhammad joined Satem in the cabin and addressed the passengers in his heavily accented English:

"Ladies and gentlemen, my name is Muhammad Ata. On behalf of al Qaeda, we have killed both pilots and are holding two flight attendants hostage. I suggest you not do anything stupid. Otherwise, we'll blow up this plane. Don't be afraid. We're taking you back to Boston. You're safe."

Convinced she would faint, one of the flight attendants leaned against the drink cart. When Rashid heard the clanging bottles, he smirked and shouted, "Don't move! Everybody sit at the end of the plane! Faster! I don't want to hear a word! I repeat, if you don't move, I won't hurt you. If you do, I'll kill you. I repeat, we're going back to Logan Airport."

The passengers didn't know their flight was diverted, and they were flying to their death. It was to the terrorists' advantage to keep them quiet. The passengers seemed calm.

Jay Clement was in his office on the second floor of Terminal B when he heard Muhammad making threats on American Airlines Flight 11. He immediately contacted the FBI.

"This is Floyd Lampard, chief of the FBI Airport Department. How may I help you?"

Jay relayed what he had heard.

"I'll be there as soon as possible," said Floyd. "In the meantime, try to stay in contact with the terrorists and find out what they want. Then, alert all airport checkpoints."

Jay tried to contact the airplane again but failed. A myriad of thoughts raced through his mind. How did the terrorists pass through security? How did they take over the airplane? What weapons did they have? How did they sneak them on board? How could this have happened?

Jay reached the checkpoint Sokol supervised, put his belongings on the conveyor belt, and fumed, "Around 8 this morning, several terrorists passed through this checkpoint with weapons, we don't know what kind, and hijacked American Airlines Flight 11! They say they are flying back to Boston! We don't know what they're up to This is awful! How could they have passed through security?!"

Jay's words stunned everyone. Sokol thought of his coworkers, held hostage by the terrorists whom he tried to remember. He had inspected their pocket knives and followed his supervisor's order to allow them to pass through security.

"You allowed them to pass the checkpoint, knowing they had weapons!" Jay shouted at Sokol. "Maybe not you directly, but why didn't you see the weapons on the screen? Now we are witnessing the catastrophic result: the hijacking of a plane with a hundred passengers and crew."

Sokol was speechless.

"You even stated in a letter that pocket knives, no matter the size, should not be allowed on board, and passengers should take off their shoes when they go through security. But you let these terrorists through. Who was on duty between 7:30 and 8:00 AM?"

"Me," Fatie managed to say. She looked pale and anxious. "But I swear I never saw anyone with a pocketknife."

"We'll confirm that," said Jay.

At that moment, Floyd Lempard, along with FBI agents and police officers from the K-9 unit, searched terminal B while they awaited the return of American Airlines Flight 11.

. . .

Muhammad sat at the controls while Abdul and Satem made sure no one panicked. Abdul still held Greta hostage. Satem held a perfume bottle and a lighter.

"The next time I use this lighter, I won't just burn your eyes," he said. "I'll blow up this plane."

Addressing the passengers, he said, "Please, watch what you do, and don't talk to each other. We'll land in Boston in no time."

"Amanda, calm down," said George. "We're on our way to Boston and should arrive there soon."

But Amanda almost screamed with fright when she saw Patrick and Chris's bodies.

"I am old but strong," said the doctor. "If only we could attack the terrorists! True, there are only three of them, but we don't know how to fly the plane. Besides, they will kill Greta if we make a move. Anyway, they said we're going back to Boston."

"Let's hold on a little longer," said Amanda. "Who knows how long we will be stranded here? God only knows what these terrorists want. What if no one can agree on a deal? Will they take us to another airport or blow up the plane?"

"Hey, old woman, do you want to die?" asked Satem.

The passengers immediately fell silent.

Jacqueline remembered Abdul's response to Sokol's question about his knife. He had said perhaps he could kill a chicken with it, but certainly not a person. When Abdul boarded the plane, Jacqueline had thought she recognized him and had asked him if he was the passenger with the knife. He had just looked at her without saying a word. How could she have been so naiv? Sokol had been right not to trust Abdul who had just killed Chris and Patrick with that very knife, taken control of the plane, and held Jacqueline's and Emma's lives in his hands. He could kill them any time. Jacqueline wanted to scream but kept quiet. She leaned against a seat, took out her phone, and dialed Steve's number. She was afraid someone might catch her, but then she saw almost all the passengers texting their loved ones.

"My name is Frank, and I am a screenwriter. I had planned to go to Los Angeles next week, but the producer convinced me to go earlier because he is busy next week. We needed to discuss some issues as soon as possible."

"My name is Robert, and I am a mechanical engineer in Boston. I was going to my friend's 40th birthday party. How could we have known the guys talking about the Islamic terrorists were the terrorists themselves? Let's hope everything ends well."

Frank tried to comfort Robert.

"What if we attacked them," he said. "There are only two of them."

"I was thinking the same thing," said Robert, "but one of them is holding that poor woman hostage."

"You're right," said Frank. "But if we attacked them, only two people would die."

"Let's leave it to fate," said Robert. "We are going back to Boston."

In his office at CNN headquarters in New York, Steve waited for Jacqueline to call and tell him about the toast and good wishes for their wedding. Jim, Steve's office mate, was reading something on his computer.

"Good job," he said. "I really like this project and your title, *The Eastern Communist Block's Journey Toward the Atlantic.* I like the part about Soviet immigrants, especially the one you named Gulliver. I also like your detailed description of the fall of Communism in the Soviet Union, Poland, Hungary, Romania, and little Albania."

Steve was flattered.

"Thank you," he said. "As I worked on the project, I remembered a Soviet diplomat I interviewed several years ago, a huge fan of communism. He defended the regime and claimed Communism would triumph over capitalism. I saw him a few days ago. I hardly recognized him. He had lost a lot of weight and didn't look well."

"Did you talk to him?" asked Jim.

"Yes," said Steve. "I asked him if he was here as a tourist. He said he had come to America as an economic immigrant. He thought his country would become heaven when in reality, it became hell. The diplomat smirked as he spoke. Now look at us, he said. We're beggars in capitalist countries. I am going to interview him as well as Sokol Kama."

"Didn't you interview him when you interviewed the Albanian window cleaners at the Twin Towers?"

"Yes, I did. Sokol works with Jacqueline, and I invited him to our wedding."

Just then, Steve's cell phone rang, and his face shone.

"That must be Jacqueline. I was expecting her call. She is flying from Boston to LA."

He knew something was wrong as soon as he heard her voice. She didn't talk with excitement about a toast. Instead, she spoke slowly, as if she feared for her life. Her words came out as surreal jibberish which Steve repeated mechanically. His heart shattered into a million pieces.

"What!!? The terrorists killed both pilots? They cut their throats with a pocket knife?! They hijacked the plane? You are flying back to Boston?"

He could not believe his ears.

"The terrorists will probably demand the release of prisoners, being held in the US. Just stay calm, okay?"

"I don't think we're going back to Boston," said Jacqueline. "If we were, the sun wouldn't be hitting the right side of the plane. I think we're still flying west."

Steve tried to reassure her.

"The terrorists are not experienced pilots so they're still figuring out how the plane works. They'll probably have everything under control in a matter of minutes. Before you know it, you'll be back in Boston. In the meantime, I'll call Jay Clement at the FAA. Then I'll call you back."

"No," she said, terrified. "I'll call you. I don't want the terrorists to know I called someone."

"All right, Honey," said Steve. "Everything's going to be okay, I promise."

Stunned, he hung up the phone.

"Did you hear that, Jim?"

Jim sat in silence, his eyes closed. Then he took out a small book and searched for Jay's number.

. . .

Fatie, Sokol, Jay, Floyd, and Gary watched the security camera video, which showed the inside of every bag on the conveyor belt, but they didn't see any knives or other weapons. Gary worried his company could lose its contract with the airport which would mean a loss of hundreds and thousands of dollars. How could Sokol and Fatie have let this happen? he thought.

Steve called Jay and told him about his conversation with Jacqueline.

"How is it possible there are no other weapons besides a couple of pocket knives?!" Jay shouted in disbelief.

He apologized to Sokol and Fatie for having accused them of negligence.

"I feel so ashamed," he said.

Jay's words took the weight of the world off Sokol's and Fatie's shoulders. Soon, Jay and Floyd left the checkpoint.

"How could the terrorists have killed two pilots and held everyone else hostage with only two small pocket knives?" Jay asked, shaking his head.

He wanted Floyd's opinion, but a myriad of thoughts raced through his mind.

"Well," he said finally, "We now know it is possible."

"What do you think they'll do now? Will they really go back to Boston or do they have some other sick plan?"

Gary followed Fatie and Sokol as they left the room.

"Thank God this wasn't your fault. Otherwise, I would have lost the contract and hundreds of thousands of dollars."

"But they still got through security with those knives," said Fatie.

"Yes, but that wasn't our fault," said Gary with a smile. It was Jay and the FBI who allowed the terrorists to take the knives on board. Now they must suffer the consequences."

"Can you believe him?" said Sokol. "Two pilots are dead, the lives of our friends and other passengers are in danger, and the only thing he cares about is his business."

"He really is something," said Fatie.

Abdul continued to hold the knife against Greta's throat. He had held it there for so long his fingers had grown numb. He felt her breath on his hands and goosebumps on her body. He recalled the many animals he had killed and which his wife had cooked for dinner. He also remembered his firstborn child who had filled the house with joy and laughter after his parents' passing.

Greta didn't dare speak. This flight, her first one, was likely her last one. But hope never dies. Her moans expressed her desire to live. But in a matter of minutes, Abdul would fulfill his promise to bin Laden, Muhammad's messenger on Earth, son of the Great Allah. He would go to heaven with Muhammad, Satem, Rashid, and Vail. He wished his wife and two-year-old son could join him. He could almost hear his wife calling, "Abdul, where are you? Come meet your son. He doesn't know you, but he calls for you and wants you to come home! Don't you hear him calling you?"

At the same time, another voice penetrated the depths of his soul: "You fool! Where is this paradise you believe in but doubt at the same time. You have questioned it ever since you were little. You listened to the Imam's preaching about the afterlife and had so many questions. You wondered if it was the same as here with rivers, oceans, and people. Does it really last an eternity, you wondered. But you pushed these questions aside because you were afraid to ask them. And now you are scared because you think you're going to heaven, but all you can hear is my voice telling you there is no heaven. None of you are going to heaven."

Abdul sighed. He looked at the passengers in front of him, and they stared back at him and the other terrorists. Although they were scared, their eyes shone with the hope everything would soon return to normal. Abdul came to himself when Greta attempted to break free.

"A demon has possessed you," said Satem. "Muhammad was right to doubt you. You are going to die, and on Judgment Day, I will make sure you end up in hell."

Marvan contacted Muhammad.

"Brother Muhammad," he exclaimed, "we took control of the

other plane and are flying right behind you toward the Twin Towers, where Jaser is waiting for us!"

Marvan was proud to be part of the Al Qaeda soldiers who had promised to destroy the West in general and America in particular.

"The time has come for us to go to heaven, to enter the world of immortality," he thought. "We deserve it. We gave our word to bin Laden, Allah's messenger, came to America, and learned how to fly. We will inflict wounds which will never heal. Yes, Professor Perkins, at the University of Hamburg, you taught us about the world's fascination with American architecture, characterized by tall buildings with many floors. You even showed us the amazing design of the Twin Towers and introduced me to the blond architect, whom I wished would have fallen in love with me so I could have made her life miserable. You were passionate about your subject and said Americans designed the best buildings. But, kind sir, you forgot about ancient Arab architecture with its beautiful mosques. Do you think one day Europe and the rest of the world will dominate us just as part of Europe once made up part of the Arabian Caliphate of Baghdad? Just you wait, the Twin Towers are about to become the largest graveyard known to man."

The plane flew below the clouds, and the passengers had a breathtaking view of New York City. They could see the Statue of Liberty as well as the gigantic Twin Towers.

An inner voice said to Abdul, "I feel bad for you! You and your Muslim friends are not going to heaven." At the same time, Abdul could hear bin Laden cursing him and putting spells on him: "Your wife and your son are going to hell, you hear me! The three of you are going to hell! You have betrayed our beautiful religion. You still have time to repay me and our brothers by killing every person on this plane."

While Abdul was processing these words, the other voice said, "You and your friends are going to die, and there's no coming back. You are about to leave this world without saying good-bye to your wife and son, who is eager to meet you."

Prompted by the voices in his head, Abdul pushed Greta away, ran into the cabin, and stabbed Muhammad twice in the throat. While he screamed in agony, Abdul shouted at the passengers they weren't flying back to Boston, but straight into the Twin Towers. They were going to die.

Muhammad realized Abdul had broken his promise to Allah and had therefore become an enemy. He wanted to take control of the plane, land it safely, and turn himself in to the authorities, for which he would serve the minimum sentence. Though blood gushed from his throat, Muhammad refused to relinquish the controls. He charged full speed ahead toward the first tower while Marvan headed for the second. Satem struck the back of Abdul's head multiple times with the bottle until he collapsed and lay motionless on the floor. George, Amanda, and other passengers rushed to his side, but it was too late. Incredulous, Jacqueline joined other passengers who were hitting and kicking the terrorists. Amid the commotion, she called Steve and told him the plane was not headed back to Boston. "God be with us," she said.

At that moment, Steve knew his life had changed forever. He had lost part of his soul. As he looked out the window, he could see a barely discernible, but fast approaching object on the horizon. A few seconds later, an airplane whizzed by. Jacqueline had been right. The plane was not flying into any of the airports in New York, but perhaps it would land in Philadelphia. However, it soon became clear it was charging toward the buildings in downtown Manhattan. At 8:45 AM, Jacqueline said, "We are flying into one of the Twin Towers."

"Where are you?" Steve asked. "Jacqueline?"

He would never hear her voice again.

PART III: SEPTEMBER 11, 2001 8:45 AM

As Besim finished cleaning the windows in Tower One, The fog lifted, revealing New York's breathtaking view. Some tourists took pictures of the city; others photographed Besim working. As he gradually ascended to the 107th floor, where he would cover for Marko during his break, he noticed a plane flying lower than usual. He thought it might be on maneuvers or part of a show, or maybe the pilot was drunk. When he saw it was a large passenger jet, he knew something was amiss. Marko, too, aware something was wrong, waved and shouted at the pilot to alert him he was going in the wrong direction. But in vain. Seconds later, the plane hit the upper part of the building. The entire structure shook, and when Besim pressed the button to continue his ascent, he discovered the electricity had gone out, leaving him hanging outside the building. Marko gripped the rails, and as soon as the building had stopped shaking, he ran toward the elevators to help his friend. When he and the other tourists saw they weren't working, they shouted, "Take the stairs! Take the stairs!" At that moment, the alarm sounded.

People said:

"Oh, my God, is it an earthquake?"

"No, I think a plane hit the building."

"I guess it wasn't the pilot's fault the plane hit the towers," said Marko.

"I guess not," said Besim. "This attack appears to have been planned."

"But who on earth would have done such a thing? Al Qaeda?"

"It has to be. I can't think of anyone else capable of this kind of attack."

More and more people, panicking and trying to save their lives, came down the stairs. As they ran, they pushed Besim and Marko. Marko eventually lost his balance. He and Besim fell and hit the metal grill. Besim hit his head hard, and his face was soon covered with blood. He bit his lip to suppress a scream. Marko jumped to his feet and tried to grab Besim, but Besim smiled and said, "It's too late. If you want to save yourself, leave me and run as fast as you can. That way, you'll still have a chance to avoid the flames that must be spreading on the lower floors."

"No!" cried Marko, as tears rolled down his cheeks."

"Marko, do you remember how it took me over three hours to get down from this building in 1993? I had no one to lean on like I do today. But this time is different. I am weak, so go on, save yourself."

Besim's words sounded like an order. Marko cried as Besim grabbed his arm and bid him farewell. He embraced his friend and turned around, but Besim shouted, "Go, Marko, just go!"

In the midst of the chaos, Besim took out his cell phone.

Marta was getting ready for work when the phone rang. She answered it and was surprised to hear Besim's voice. He didn't normally call that time of day.

"Marta, are you alone? Is Trim with you?"

"He's in his room. Why?"

"I need you to be strong. The Twin Towers were attacked, and Al Qaeda is likely responsible."

Marta almost cried.

"I just told you to be strong, didn't I?"

She bit her lip.

"Now listen carefully."

Besim told her what happened. Marta bit her lip after every heart-breaking word and tried her best not to scream or cry.

"I won't say anything to Trim yet," she said.

Suddenly, she felt two small hands grab her from behind.

"Mommy, I just saw on the news the Twin Towers are on fire," said Trim. "Are you talking to Dad?"

Marta searched for the right words to say to her son. All at once, Trim grabbed the phone out of her hand and started talking to his father.

"Dad, you named me Trim, which means brave. I am and always will be as brave as my name. Are you in the Twin Towers?"

"Yes, Son. I am in Tower One," said Besim, caught off guard.

"We're coming to save you," said Trim.

"It's no use, Son. The towers are on fire and will collapse any time. Only the people on the lower floors have a chance. I just hope Uncle Rrok will escape. You must be strong like your mother."

Trim could no longer hold back the tears.

"Come on, Trim! You just promised me you'd be strong."

Trim instinctively grabbed his mother's hand. He wanted to go to the Twin Towers as quickly as possible to save his father. He hoped for a miracle. He felt like he was in a dream.

"All right, Dad," he said, wiping his tears with his hand. "I'll try."

Although he was young, he was mature enough to understand the situation.

"Listen carefully," Besim continued. "In a few days, you and your mother are going back to Kosovo, to my hometown of Prizren. Kosovo will be independent soon."

"Yes, Kosovo will be independent, maybe sooner than we think."

"It's incredibly beautiful. There are majestic mountains like Bjeshket e Nemura with Gjeravica the highest peak; the green fields of Fushe Kosove; crystal clear rivers like the Drin, the longest in the region; the lovely lakes in the Sharr Mountains."

"Yes, Dad." Trim could barely speak. "You told me about these places many times, and I promise I will visit them and Gruda, where Mom was born. Dad, can you hear me? Dad?"

No answer. Marta grabbed the phone.

"Besim, Besim!" she cried, but heard only loud noises and screams.

Marko was trying to get out of the building as quickly as possible. He could not stop thinking about Besim and his fiancé, and he wondered if he would ever see her again. These thoughts quickened his pace. Meanwhile, people waved white tablecloths out the windows, pleading for help while others rushed out of the building without looking back. Bystanders and firefighters lined the streets. When Marko stopped for a second, he noticed a girl praying God would save her.

"Never mind the prayers!" another girl cried, grabbing her hand. "Come with me."

But she remained motionless. She looked as if she truly saw God.

"I'm not going anywhere," she said. "God Almighty will save me. He will come and take me with Him. Stay with me, and He will save you, too."

Marko looked at her and thought, "Poor girl, she's losing her mind. Everlasting curses on the people who did this!"

"Cursed be the terrorists!" people shouted repeatedly.

"Why haven't they sent any rescue helicopters?" asked someone.

"That's a good question," someone else said. "The towers are tall enough for people to see them. Why isn't anybody coming to help us get out of here?"

The delirious crowd continued to rush down the stairs.

"Will someone think to bring a helicopter?" wondered Marko. "Why doesn't someone take us from this cursed place?"

Suddenly, sadness overwhelmed him.

"How many of the hundreds of terrified people could fit in those helicopters?" he thought.

He continued to follow the crowd down the stairs, hoping to make it out alive. He couldn't take his mind off Besim who had managed to escape seven years before when those cursed bombs had exploded on the lower floors of the tower.

The thick smoke made breathing more difficult the farther down he went, and waves of heat burned his sweat-covered face.

"It's pointless!" said a desperate, delirious voice. "The lower floors have caught fire. We have nowhere to go!"

Marko didn't want to believe their words. Although many people went back upstairs and others jumped out of windows in desperation, he pressed onward as the flames engulfed the staircase and the railings began to melt.

As he pondered what to do next, his cell phone rang. It was probably Maria. Exhausted as he was, he managed to answer it. It was indeed her. She asked in a tremulous, frightened voice where he was. How should he respond? He thought about their engagement which he had planned to announce that Sunday at Steve and Jacqueline's wedding.

"Please, Darling, tell me where you are!" Maria persisted.

"I'm far away, at the end of Liberty Street," said Marko.

"Get out of there!" said Maria in the Arberesh dialect.

Her words melted into a mournful wail.

"Talk to me, Marko Darling!"

"I'm here. We may never see each other again."

"What are you saying? Of course we'll see each other again, and we'll always be together. Come, Marko, I'm waiting for you."

Far from the fiery destruction, Maria, with her tousled dark hair, creased forehead, and sparkling, opaque eyes, understood what was happening but didn't want to believe Marko had said his last words.

Marko headed for the window. Better to jump as he had jumped many times from the high, steep rocks near San Demetrio to dive into the Ionian Sea's blue water. When he reached the surface, his friends exclaimed, "Good for you, Marko! We wouldn't dive from such high rocks!"

Now, he jumped for the last time from an even greater height and flew toward his waiting fiancé. As he fell to his death, propelled by the eddies of air which cooled his scorched face, he cried, "Maria, wait for me!", but Maria, hundreds of feet below, would have found it virtually impossible to recognize Marko among the hundreds of falling bodies.

. . .

In his office on the twenty-fifth floor, Said felt a tremor and heard an alarm when the plane hit the tower. He Instinctively jumped to his feet and waited a moment, but the alarm continued to sound. From the hallway, he heard footsteps and terrified voices. When he understood the gravity of the situation, he ran from his office and was shocked to see almost all the workers on that floor rushing toward the stairs because the elevator wasn't working. A few of them stayed where they were while others tried to return to their offices. But when someone on a cell phone shouted, "A plane has hit the tower!", hordes of people ran toward the stairs. Said couldn't believe what was happening, or rather, he didn't want to. He marveled that such a thing could happen. Suddenly, from the corridor window, he saw burning pieces fall to the ground like meteorites. Then, he knew what he had heard was true.

"Was it a deliberate attack?" he wondered.

He immediately thought of Serena. Where was she now? Maybe in her office on the twentieth floor. Or perhaps she was trying to escape and was calling him for help. But then he remembered he had taken her to the hospital and was supposed to pick her up around noon.

Where was Jaser al Sadri? Had he stayed in his office and forgotten he and Said had business to discuss? Said hurried to Jaser's office and opened the door, but no one was inside. It appeared he had escaped and had blended in with the crowd. Said would do the same.

He went to the fire escape and was relieved to see Jaser at the door. But instead of opening it, he locked it.

"Jaser, what are you doing?" cried Said.

Jaser shivered and whirled around. When he saw Said, he looked at him with wild, fiery eyes, and a devilish smile formed on his sullied lips. He pulled an iron pipe with a sharp point, which appeared to have come from an office chair leg, from his inner jacket pocket.

"What am I doing?" growled Jaser, shaking the pipe. "I'm fulfilling my obligation to Islam along with my brothers who hit this building with a plane. I locked the door so as many infidels as possible on the upper floors, including you, who, by marrying a Christian, violated our sacred laws, and me, would die."

When Said heard these words, he understood everything, and a piercing scream rose from deep within. Now he knew why Jaser avoided his glances and why his eyes darkened, as if he were concealing something behind his smiles. The attack on the Twin Towers had been the culmination of the criminals' work, supposedly in the name of Allah.

When he heard people shouting and knocking on the door, among them, likely Besim, Marko, and Rrok, Said prepared to fight Jaser.

"Come here, you slime!" fumed Jaser. "I'll kill you like a dog with this pipe. If there hadn't been a security checkpoint on the first floor, I would have brought a gun and blown everybody to bits!"

Said remained motionless, his blood frozen, and waited with bated breath. This was his first encounter with an armed man who didn't just want to rob him, but wanted to take his life, a person Said had helped and loved like a brother. But Jaser had become convinced he needed weapons not to defend himself, but to attack and kill people like Said whom he considered traitors of Islam. Said was strong and muscular, but unarmed, except for his open hands, ready to fend off the threatening pipe. Would he die just a few days before Serena was due to give birth to their daughter? No, that was out of the question.

When Jaser, chattering as if delirious, pointed the pipe at Said's left arm, his most vulnerable part, he leaned forward, turned away, and stepped back, almost losing his balance, but he persisted with his attack. Said avoided being struck by the pipe, but it scratched his forearm.

He felt a sharp pain, and blood soaked his shirt. Still, he managed to kick Jaser in the stomach. He doubled over, groaning in pain. Said jumped on him, and the two of them fell to the ground. Jaser injured his head and remained unconscious for a moment, but he didn't let go of the pipe. He raised it, and Said felt its point graze his throat. In a matter of seconds, Jaser would stab him.

Said grabbed Jaser's hand, and with his other hand, he clenched his throat and dug his nails into his smooth skin. Jaser sighed, shook his head, and let go of the pipe. Said grabbed it and stabbed him in the throat. Jaser winked, opened his mouth, and tried to stand. But shaking violently, he fell to the ground again.

While his phone rang incessantly, Said, with one hand on his bleeding wound, stood up, swayed, staggered toward the door, and forced it open. A steady stream of people passed into the corridor. Some fell, and others fell on top of them, But they picked themselves up and continued toward the stairs which led to the lower floors. Said was among them. Along the way, he saw Rrok's small, thin, bent frame. He could hardly walk. He had taken off his sweater and had wrapped it around a living being in his hand. Said approached him and asked, "Rrok, how are you feeling?"

When Rrok turned toward him, Said saw his pale, worn face, his tired, fluttering eyes, and his heaving chest. He looked like a dead man, risen from the grave.

Despite the intense pain in his forearm, Said clutched Rrok's sweater. Before he could open it, he heard the cry of a little boy, no more than a year old. He squirmed and extended his little hands toward him, as if he were his father.

"I found him at the bottom of the stairs," Rrok murmured. "I don't know his parents."

"How awful!" thought Said. "Will anyone find them? Will they escape this chaos?"

Although he was safe, the boy continued to cry.

"Do you have any idea where Besim and Marko are?" asked Said as they continued their difficult descent.

Rrok could only lift his eyes. He could not and didn't even try to hold back the tears which trickled down his face. At that moment, Said understood everything. Marko and Besim had remained on the upper floors from where it would have been virtually impossible to escape.

Said's telephone, which had remained silent for a few minutes, started ringing again. Holding the boy, who, to his astonishment had stopped crying, Said answered it and heard Serena's voice. After she had heard about the World Trade Center attack on the news, she had cut her hospital appointment short. A doctor had taken her to Liberty Street, where she, Maria, and thousands of others waited to learn the fate of their loved ones. The crowd even tried to cut through the long line of police officers who could barely control them.

"Oh, Said, thank God I reached you! Where are you?" asked Serena.

"I'm on my way downstairs. I should reach the exit soon."

"Are you all right, Darling? You sound tired."

Said wasn't sure how to respond.

"I'm fine. I told you, I'll see you soon."

But he didn't know when or if he would see her. Still, he hoped he would see her. He didn't know how he arrived in the lobby of Tower 1 and walked through it with Rrok following him, barely able to move. He was sure the tower would collapse and bury them both alive. Said and Rrok exited the building and continued their interminable walk toward the street, inundated with people coming out of the World Trade Center, Deutsche Bank, and an Orthodox church. They went as far away as possible from the building.

At some point, Rrok stopped. When Said lost sight of him, he turned around and saw his eyes roll back in his head, he foamed at the mouth, his face turned ashen, and his breathing grew shallow.

"Hold on just a little longer," said Said, looking toward the burning building.

The crackling flames had almost reached the center of the tower, and smoke rose in the sky.

Rrok took a few effortful and unsteady steps forward. Said, with the child in his arms, ran toward him. Rrok gave Said an apologetic look and collapsed.

"Save yourself, Said," he managed to say. "I can't go any farther. The tower could fall any minute, and pieces could hit you. It could become your and this poor orphan's grave. The child must live."

Said bent over him, put an arm around him, and tried to lift him to his feet.

"I told you," Rrok moaned, so exhausted his words came out as broken syllables, "save yourself. You have a family. Your wife will give birth soon. No one's waiting for me except my niece, Marta. It wasn't a given I would go back to Gruda or that Besim would go back to Kosovo."

He tried to say more and open his fluttering eyes, but he couldn't. He lay there, motionless, as if he were sleeping.

Said bit his lip to contain his overwhelming sorrow. Just as Marko had tried to save Besim, so, too, Said had tried to save Rrok from the lava which gushed from the tower's ruins and swallowed everything in its path. With a heavy heart, Said fled from that scene of death. His phone rang. He barely managed to answer it. It was his wife again.

"Serena," he said, "I'm at the end of Liberty Street."

"Turn right. I'll wave my handkerchief," she said.

Said did as directed.

Jacqueline's last words echoed within Steve. He felt as if he were having a nightmare from which he would soon awaken with a sigh of relief. When he told Jacqueline about it, she would throw herself into the shelter of his strong arms. But this wasn't a bad dream.

"I want to go to the tower," Steve told Jim.

Jim felt numb and didn't know what to say.

"I know you're surprised, but who knows? Maybe Jacqueline and her friends are alive."

Jim could barely contain a deep sigh.

"She can't be dead! These days, brides can't die a few days before their weddings. Isn't that right, Jim?"

Steve's eyes lit up and his face sparkled like the sun at dawn. Putting his hands on his friend's shoulders, he chided him.

"Why don't you answer me?"

Steve almost left the office and went to the tower, but the phone's sharp ring brought him back to reality. He heard the voice of CNN's general director, filled with emotion, as if in a fog, who told him to go with some cameramen to Liberty Street to report on the event which had brought America to its knees.

"Please understand," he said. "Since you're busy with your documentary about immigrants from the East, I wanted to give this job to someone else, but this tragedy traumatized almost all of our journalists. You, on the other hand, are more laid back and more experienced. I know you're getting married on Sunday, and you're thinking about Jacqueline. The things you'll see and describe will break your heart, but afterwards, she will comfort you. Therefore, I beg you, please accept this assignment."

Steve could barely contain a scream. He wanted to tell the director he was the only journalist who had the right not to be disturbed. He wanted to tell him Jacqueline could not console him because she had died on one of the planes that hit the Towers. But he couldn't.

"Do you hear me, Steve? Don't wait. Go there as soon as possible," said the director.

Jim wanted to tell the general director what had happened, but Steve motioned for him to keep quiet.

"I'm on my way now," he said, choking back a sob.

"You and Jim will do the report together," said the director.

"He's right here in the office," said Steve.

"All right," said the director.

Steve hung up the phone. The light in his eyes had faded. In a surprisingly calm voice, he said, "Let's go, Jim. Let's do this for Jacqueline, her friends, and everyone else who died in this horrible attack."

Jay and Floyd reflected on the day's events. In one of the worst terrorist attacks, American Airlines Flight 11, with 98 passengers, several flight attendants, and two pilots, had struck the North Tower of the World Trade Center in New York like a giant missile. The passengers and crew, along with hundreds of people in the building, perished. The terrorists sacrificed their lives for their warped cause. Only the murderous mind of bin Laden could have devised such a devilish plan. But was this monstrous attack really caused by pocket knives?

Floyd felt uneasy as he hurried to his office where other FBI agents had started their investigation. He asked a colleague for the list of passengers on American Airlines Flight 11.

"How could this have happened?" he wondered.

He sighed as he watched Steve's report. When he saw the second plane hit the South Tower at 9:03 AM, he froze, for he now understood the extent to which the terrorists had planned their attack.

The phone rang. Jay called to say the FAA had just ordered the closure of every airport in America.

"How awful!" sighed Floyd, who was approaching seventy. He had worked for the FBI for forty years and had risen in the ranks to become the department head at Logan Airport. This was the first tragedy of its kind in the history of American aviation. He became more and more convinced bin Laden had masterminded the attack. Had he planned more? The question gnawed at his soul.

He requested the list of passengers on the second plane. He looked at his watch. It was almost 9:43. He kept his eyes glued to the television. Steve's report was interspersed with news updates from the CNN studio. Another American Airlines plane, Flight 77, which had taken off from New Jersey, crashed into the Pentagon. Floyd jumped as if bitten by a snake. Bin Laden's terrorists had attacked the brain and pride of the American Army. The news commentator said the White House was evacuated within a matter of minutes. But where was President Bush? Floyd couldn't remember until later that day when he saw him on TV, speaking in Florida. He didn't look like the president, but like an image of him. He had ordered military forces, police officers, and FBI agents to guard Logan International Airport. In the terminals, soldiers drew their automatic weapons, and dogs stood, ready to attack anyone suspicious.

Time passed slowly. Later, the CNN commentator reported that all federal buildings in Washington were being evacuated. Meanwhile, Floyd's assistant brought him the list of passengers from the plane which had crashed into the Pentagon. His eyes wandered over the names of hundreds of people, no longer among the living. He paused whenever he encountered names of Arabs and suspected every plane had several, but in the three lists, he didn't find more than five such names. How had a small group subdued a large number of passengers? Why hadn't the passengers been able to stop the terrorists? Were they working with terrorists from other countries? It was a mystery.

At 10:25, Floyd saw the South Tower fall, burning up hundreds of people, as if it were a large cardboard crematorium. Five minutes later, CNN reported the fall of sections of the Pentagon. A wail rose within Floyd.

Then came more shocking news. United Airlines Flight 93, flying from Newark Liberty International Airport to Washington, had crashed near Pittsburgh, Pennsylvania. Perhaps it had been an accident, unrelated to the terrorist attacks. Floyd called the president of United Airlines. The news of the crash broke his heart. Floyd wondered why the plane hadn't hit a building.

He requested the passenger list for the United flight and received it without delay. To his amazement, he discovered the names of four Arabs. Either they weren't part of the terrorist plot or passengers had fought them.

Floyd left his office and hurried downstairs to the security checkpoint.

At 10:28 AM, the North Tower fell, swallowing hundreds of people. Steve and Jim continued to cover the tragedy which would forever remain in the annals of history. They showed pictures of people who had come out of the Twin Towers, surrounding skyscrapers, stores, restaurants, and cafes. Ambulances with doctors and nurses arrived on the scene, and civilians risked their lives to rescue people from the suffocating smoke, swallowing everything in its path. Police officers guarded the area, and firefighters pulled victims from the rubble.

Meanwhile, Steve recalled a radio reporter from Chicago named Herbert Harrison, who on May 6, 1937, covered the arrival of the Hindenburg at New York's airport. The giant German balloon had departed from Frankfurt, flown across the Atlantic Ocean and was supposed to land in New York. Steve could still see the pictures of the Hindenburg's majestic, carefree flight and the thousands of spectators who had come to watch it land, but had seen it crash instead. The terrified passengers, unable to escape the tongues of fire which engulfed the balloon, jumped to their death just like the people on the upper floors of the Twin Towers, who saw no other alternative. Steve recalled Herbert Harrison's words about the crash which took the lives of thirty-four of the balloon's ninety-eight passengers: "What fire! What ruin! This is the world's worst disaster." What would the attack on the Twin Towers be called? Within two hours, hundreds of people had died, and when all was said and done, thousands more would likely perish. Years ago, when Steve watched the documentary which made Herbert Harrison famous, he dreamed of achieving that kind of success, but not by reporting on a tragedy. His anger and bitterness formed his words.

He interviewed people on the lower floors who had managed to escape. They told him how they felt as they descended the stairs to get away from the grave which had opened like a volcanic crater and had buried scores of people, including friends they couldn't save. One person talked about the hundreds of people, including acquaintances, who had stayed on the upper floors of the North Tower and had said their final good-byes to him on the phone. Steve mentioned Besim, Marko, and Rrok. Someone shook his head with sadness and said they were window washers.

At that moment, Steve saw Said on the other side of the street, holding something in his jacket, and a young woman waiting for him with open arms. She also saw Steve. It was Serena, Said's pregnant wife. Steve was glad Said and Serena had survived. Said took the child, whom Rrok had rescued, from his jacket, and handed him to Serena, who took him in her loving arms.

Steve surmised Serena had been far away from the towers when the attacks occurred and went back to wait for Said when she heard what had happened. Said looked like he had lived through a nightmare. In his report, Steve included pictures of Said, running toward Serena, about to give birth in the midst of death. If only Jacqueline were running toward Steve! Steve cried inwardly as he often did during this trying time, but he kept his composure with superhuman strength.

As a child in 1966, he had heard about the construction of the towers which became the World Trade Center. The first tower was completed in 1970, and the second one was completed two years later. Over 10,000 people worked on the towers, and 60 workers died during their construction. The residents of New York watched with pride as the buildings rose and felt as if they were watching twins grow. What had taken years to build was destroyed within three hours.

As Steve, Jim, and their cameraman walked to their car, Steve's telephone rang. It was the director of information at CNN, who, on behalf of all the department heads, offered his heartfelt thanks to him and his colleague for expressing America's pain, and he told Steve to go home and rest. Steve could barely contain a sob and almost told the director he had lost Jacqueline in the attack.

The car drove through the wide, straight streets of New York and past skyscrapers with their fragile windows, which, although they glistened in the September sun, seemed to mourn their fallen sisters. The people, who wandered the streets, grieved, too.

Steve asked the chauffeur to go to the Park Plaza Hotel.

"Oh, that's the hotel where you and Jacqueline were supposed to get married," he murmured. "How awful for you!"

Steve clenched his jaw to suppress a blood-curdling scream which could not possibly have alleviated his sorrow. When the car stopped in front of the large hotel, Jim asked, "Do you want me to come with you?"

"No, thank you," said Steve.

Jim embraced him. He knew time alone in the hall where he and Jacqueline were supposed to have had their wedding would help Steve regain his composure. Jim looked at him with compassion as he slowly walked toward the stairs.

In one of the offices of American Airlines, an assistant handed Floyd a suitcase.

"This belonged to an Egyptian passenger, Muhammad Ata," said the assistant. "It appears not to have made it onto Flight 11 because of a delay in Portland"

"Aha!" Floyd thought. "Muhammad Ata and his friends went to Portland the night before to cover their tracks. They came from there to Boston and got on American Airlines flight 11. Muhammad Ata had already purchased tickets for them". His suspicions were confirmed when he talked to company supervisors. Both Muhammad Ata and Abdul al Ramzi had flown from Portland to Boston. When Floyd opened the suitcase, he found pilot uniforms and a letter in Arabic. He wondered if the terrorists had packed the uniforms in case they had needed to disguise themselves. He asked FBI agents to find translators, who could read Arabic, and to learn as much as they could about the terrorists. It was clear they had intended to hit the Twin Towers and the Pentagon. But the fourth plane, which crashed in Pennsylvania? Where had it been headed?

Floyd's assistant returned with the translation of the letter, found in Muhammad Ata's suitcase. As he read it, he flashed his eyes, and his hands trembled:

"Don't worry. For we, Allah's devoted children and members of al Qaeda, founded by holy bin Laden, will soon be in heaven. Check your weapons before you leave. Hold on to your knives, and don't let those animals get you down."

To whom did Muhammad Ata address his letter? To himself or his friends?

Floyd knew these fundamentalist fanatics were not afraid to die since they believed they would enter Paradise. How could they have believed such nonsense? The "animals" referred to the poor passengers who had died on the planes. The terrorists probably called them other names as well. The words "hold on to your knives" proved they had used weapons other than firearms.

After reading the letter, Floyd left the American Airlines office, looked for Jay, and found him near the security checkpoint in Terminal B. He looked somber. Floyd showed him the letter. As he read it, he sighed, and his eyes darkened.

"Obviously, the terrorists used knives to kill the crew members," he said. "But how long were they?"

"They were pocket knives, smaller than your badge," said Floyd.

Incredulous, Jay lifted his badge.

"But how could they have killed the pilots and flight attendants with only pocket knives?" he wondered.

He bit his lip, squinted, grabbed Floyd's arm, and invited him to sit down. A few passengers, who thought their canceled flights would depart later, stood nearby.

"I'm convinced the terrorists didn't just use pocket knives," said Floyd. "I think they used other objects as well."

"For God's sake, what are you talking about?" Jay demanded, putting a hand on his reddish hair.

"They also used glass bottles and perfume bottles," said Floyd.

Jay's eyes widened. He knitted his twitching brow and clenched his fists.

"Let me explain. The terrorists had the type of pocket knives, allowed by the FAA. Since they were smaller than a badge, They made it through security without a problem."

Jay recalled his conversation in May with the Albanian head of security, Sokol Kama.

"In addition," continued Floyd, "they had large bottles with alcoholic beverages and perfume bottles with tear gas."

Jay also recalled the letter Sokol had written, in which he had said neither small pocket knives nor bottles should be allowed on board. Not only Sokol, but also passengers and some of the airport workers had made the same recommendation, but he had done nothing.

"Spraying a robber two or three times in the eyes will blind him, at least for a few minutes."

"That's true," said Jay. "The terrorists probably sprayed the two flight attendants in first class."

"Exactly. The two terrorists in second class probably did the same. Then, they pulled out their knives, grabbed the flight attendants, held the blades to their throats, and threatened to kill them if the passengers moved from their seats."

Floyd's eyes bore into Jay.

"What were the poor passengers supposed to do? Attack the terrorists?" he said in a guttural voice.

"As I told you before, we heard the voice of Muhammad Ata, apparently, the leader of the terrorists. In an attempt to reassure the passengers, he told them they were returning to Boston, and he threatened to kill them and crash the plane if they moved."

"Exactly. And as a result, the passengers thought the plane would land here, and the terrorists would negotiate with government officials, as often happened. The passengers on the other planes thought the same thing."

"But how did they kill the pilots?"

Floyd knit his brow and shrugged his shoulders.

"I'm not sure. They may have feigned panic, knocked on the cockpit door, and requested help for a flight attendant who had fainted or suffered another crisis. What would the co-pilot have done?"

Without waiting for an answer, Floyd continued: "He would have come out of the cockpit. And that's probably what he did. Then, one of the terrorists, hiding behind the door, probably struck the back of his head with a glass bottle. The co-pilot may have fallen to the floor, unconscious. Once he fell, the terrorist likely stabbed him and left his corpse there. The pilot, concerned, probably left the cockpit and suffered the same fate."

Jay agreed with Floyd's suppositions.

"The terrorists probably scared the passengers into submission by threatening to blow up the plane if they disobeyed their orders."

In short, the passengers assumed the two planes were returning to Logan International Airport in Boston. They didn't know the planes were flying into the Twin Towers. By the time they understood what was happening, it was too late to stop the terrorists.

"What about the plane that crashed near Pittsburgh?" Jay asked.

Wrinkling his brow, Floyd thought long and hard.

"You told me Steve informed you that his fiancé, who was on American Airlines Flight 11, called him and told him what was happening. It's possible relatives of the passengers called them and told them two planes had crashed into the Twin Towers and warned them their plane could crash into a building, too."

"And as a result, many passengers, aware of their precarious situation, attacked the terrorists who had taken control of the plane. The terrorist, flying the plane, probably lost control, and the plane crashed before it had reached its destination."

"You're probably right."

"What was their target? The White House perhaps?"

Floyd rubbed his wrinkled face and shrugged his shoulders.

"That wouldn't surprise me," he said, his brow darkening.

"Just awful!" sighed Jay.

Meanwhile, Floyd's assistant approached him.

"Here's some information about Muhammad Ata," he said, handing him several papers which he read with eagerness. Floyd summarized their content for Jay:

"He studied architecture in Cairo and Hamburg. He came to the US in 2000. He and some friends went to the Hufmann Aviation School in Venice, Florida to become pilots. Muhammad Ata paid 40,000 dollars for the courses. At that time, the CIA didn't suspect anything. On August 4, 2001, he was in Orlando, Florida. That's how he covered his tracks. Yesterday, he went from Boston to Portland with Abdul al Ramzi and this morning, as you know, he came back to join his cohorts."

Floyd handed Jay the list with the names of the Arabs on the four planes, pulverized along with them.

Jay felt as if part of his heart had been ripped out of him.

"They came to our country, studied to become pilots in our country, and killed us with our own planes," he sighed.

Floyd wanted to speak but kept silent.

While they were immersed in conversation, CNN broadcast an interview with experts, who, in hushed, tremulous tones, discussed the history of hijackings. The first hijacking occurred in 1968, when Palestinian terrorists forced an El Al plane, which had departed from Rome, to land in Algiers and demanded the release of several Arab prisoners. The experts also mentioned hijackings in 1970, 1976, and 1981. The worst tragedy occurred in 1985 at the Cairo airport, when Egyptian soldiers attacked a plane, hijacked by Palestinians. They killed not only the terrorists, but also fifty-two passengers. In March of 2001, at the Medina airport, Saudi snipers attacked a Russian plane, en route to Istanbul, which had been hijacked by Chechnyan terrorists. Three terrorists and a flight attendant were killed.

The hijackings, which had occurred just a short time ago, differed from earlier hijackings in that they not only caused the death of the terrorists and passengers on the planes, but, Worst of all, they led to the destruction of the Twin Towers, burying hundreds of people in the rubble. Each plane, carrying about one hundred tons of fuel and traveling at more than 500 miles an hour, became a weapon with as much energy as a small atomic bomb. The extreme heat melted the towers' steel structures, causing them to fall.

The experts predicted the death toll could rise to around two- or three thousand.

"It's an immense loss," said one commentator, a military historian. "During the Korean War, which lasted from 1950-1954, we lost almost 34,000 soldiers. During the Vietnam War, which lasted eleven years, from 1964-1975, we lost almost 59,000 soldiers. In this case, we don't have an exact number, but we may be talking hundreds or thousands, I hope to God fewer people killed within a few hours."

The commentator shook his head and closed his eyes, barely able to breathe. He forgot millions of people were waching him not only in America, but all over the world. Still, he had a right to feel the way he did. The indignant spectators shook their heads, too for the dead were people like them: workers and tourists, savoring the magical view of the city from dizzying heights.

"Oh, God!" sighed Jay. "Thousands of soldiers gave their lives in wars which lasted years while scores of people in the towers perished in a matter of minutes. It reminds me of that December morning in 1941 when Japanese planes attacked Pearl Harbor. In a short time, more than three thousand of our sons died before they could realize their dreams."

"The people on the planes and in the towers had dreams, too!" Floyd gasped. "Some of them had just started a new work day, some were traveling."

Gray-haired Floyd could no longer contain his sobs.

"Imagine the greetings, wishes, and messages people shared over the phone not only in New York, but in other American cities as well! Think of the meetings young lovers arranged, the women who told their husbands they were pregnant, the engagements and weddings that had been planned, like Steve Ferguson's wedding which was supposed to happen this Sunday. He called you first because he wanted to tell you what had happened to Jacqueline. He was able to keep his composure while reporting on the attack of the Twin Towers."

"Many people talked and smiled even as the planes hit the towers," said Jay. "Others worked, their eyes glued to their computers or documents on their desks. They sipped coffee, ate, told stories. Young men and women whispered words of love to each other, maybe for the first time, and brushed their lips against each other. Maybe they were hesitant to kiss since it was their first one. Little did they know it would be their last. They never imagined those planes would land on them."

Jay's eyes glistened with tears.

"Perhaps some people fainted or cried out, unable to put their fear into words," sighed Floyd, swallowing the horror that ate him through and through.

"How many families are mourning their loved ones, lost on the planes and in the towers?" sighed Jay, his eyes filled with grief. "Why? Why?"

He answered his own question.

"Because we at the FAA didn't do our job. We should never have allowed passengers to carry pocket knives, bottles, or lighters. Also, we should have checked their shoes where they could have hidden explosives."

He sighed and almost whispered, "This tragedy happened because we failed to do our job."

Floyd's eyes fell as he stammered, "We, more than anyone, are responsible for what happened."

Jay shrugged his shoulders.

"What do you mean?"

"You mentioned the terrorists trained in this country to become pilots and attacked us with our planes. Right?"

Jay nodded.

"A few weeks ago, one of my colleagues in New York told me in early July, an agent in Phoenix named Kenneth Williams sent him a memo in which he stated some young Arabs were taking courses to learn how to fly commercial planes, perhaps with the support of Osama bin Laden, in preparation for an eventual attack."

"Really?" Jay exclaimed. "What did your colleagues do when they got the memo?"

Floyd smiled bitterly and looked solemn.

"No one even bothered to look at it."

"Unbelievable!" sighed Jay, his face pale.

"I didn't give it much thought, either. If I had insisted the head of the New York office put those Arabs under surveillance, I'm convinced the FBI would have found them, thereby avoiding this horror. That's why I say we, more than anyone, were responsible for this tragedy."

A tense silence fell. Finally, Jay spoke, on the verge of tears.

"We at the FAA bear a greater responsibility for what happened. If we hadn't allowed the aforementioned objects on board, we would have nipped this tragedy in the bud."

Without waiting for an answer, Jay stood up and almost staggered to the security checkpoint near which Sokol was talking to a passenger who insisted the flights, suspended for an indefinite period, should be rescheduled for the next day. He barely managed to break away from the unruly passenger. When he entered the checkpoint, Sokol found himself face to face with Jay. He did not understand the look in his eyes, brimming with tears, until Jay approached him, put a hand on his shoulder, and said, "Forgive me."

With his words, he apologized to Sokol for disregarding his suggestions and for not answering the letter he had written several months ago. At the same time, he apologized to the other employees who had recommended more or less the same changes.

Sokol did not feel the need to respond to Jay's apology.

"This evil came from people from the east!" shouted the passenger with whom Sokol had just spoken. He was a businessman, who was apparently supposed to go to Florida for a pressing matter. Rather tall and with a withered face, he paced the area around the security checkpoint, not seeming to care about what had happened in the Twin Towers and elsewhere. His ranting shocked everyone around him, but not Fatie. Small as she was, she confronted the man, who regarded her with wide eyes.

"Sir, I am from the East," she said, eyeing him with contempt.

Her voice sounded withdrawn, as if at any moment, it would break from the sorrow she felt for herself and her friends.

"I am from Afghanistan, suffering under the cruel yoke of the Taliban. I escaped from there with the help of the International Red Cross. They brought me to America, my second home. Maybe I'm a bad person."

Fatie paused, keeping her eyes on the stunned businessman. Then, pointing to a slender woman with a cleaning cart, she continued more passionately:

"Maybe the cleaner from Indonesia is a bad person. Unfortunately,

Indonesia has Islamic fundamentalists who have nothing to do with true believers like me. In fact, we hate them."

Fatie pointed to a middle-aged man and his wife at the restaurant counter.

"Maybe that husband and wife from Morocco are bad people. Maybe my friend who works with me in security is a bad person. He came from Albania, a country in the East, where Muslims, Catholics, and Orthodox Christians live in peace."

Fatie laid a hand on Sokol's shoulder. She spoke in rapid, broken English. Even if people didn't understand her, they understood her broken spirit. Therefore, no one made fun of her or interrupted her.

The businessman wanted to say something, but before he could open his mouth, Floyd grabbed his arm and took him away.

"What happened today could happen again," said Fatie, her flaming eyes taking in everyone around her. "Indeed, evil comes from the East, from one man, Osama bin Laden, who hides in the mountains of Afghanistan and feeds a few thousand shortsighted fanatics with hatred of the West in general and America in particular."

When they saw Osama bin Laden, the al Qaeda members, who sat crosslegged on the plain, jumped to their feet, raised their Kalashnikovs, and shouted, "Bin Laden! Bin Laden!"

Bin Laden watched their faces. The majority had beards, but a few had mustaches. Some of the younger men did not yet have facial hair. Turbans covered the people's burning heads, flaming cheeks, fiery eyes, and innocent lips. They looked at bin Laden as if he were Allah himself, come from heaven to bless them.

Bin Laden's penetrating eyes shone with pride. He looked to his right, where Khalid Sheik Muhammad sat.

"I have good news for you, my children," he said, opening his arms. "I just learned that some of our loyal followers, who are now in heaven, took the planes from nonbelieving pilots and destroyed the Twin Towers in New York, the pride of America. Hundreds, I hope to God, even thousands of people were buried alive."

When the frenzied crowd heard these words, they chanted, "Bin Laden! Bin Laden!"

Their shouts echoed throughout the surrounding hills and mountains.

"We need to thank this man right here," said bin Laden. "You know who he is."

"Khalid Sheik Muhammad," cried voices from the crowd.

"Exactly. Allah helped him give me the idea which brothers like you made a reality."

Bin Laden raised Khalid's arm. His eyes darkened as he recalled the night they planned to attack the Twin Towers.,

He had remained speechless when Khalid, with his dark, penetrating raven eyes, which fluttered under his thick eyebrows, had told him, in a godly voice, how to proceed. Bin Laden, who understood mathematics, mechanics, and science, had never thought of doing what Khalid proposed. People called him a mastermind, but in fact, Khalid was the mastermind.

Bin Laden beamed with pride.

"My sons, are you ready to follow in their footsteps?" shouted Khalid. "Are you ready to go to heaven with those martyrs? Shouted bin Laden, his eyes so wide they almost burst.

The delirious people raised their Kalashnikovs and cried, "We're ready! Muhammad has sent you to us! Tell us what we must do to receive our reward!"

"I thank you from the bottom of my heart. I knew you would answer me thus. We will continue our Jihad. We will fight the infidels. We'll bomb men, women, and children wherever they are: at home, in bed. You will strap bombs to your waists in train stations, bus stations, hotels, anywhere with a lot of people. You'll blow yourselves up with them. Then, Allah will send you to heaven. Unlike the American and Western European infidels, we love that kind of death more than they love life. So, are you ready to die?"

Voices from the crowd shouted, "Point to us , O great Bin Laden, and we'll go wherever you want!"

"Choose me!"

"Choose me!"

"Choose all of us!"

The people blushed and drooled, and their eyes seemed to bleed. As the crowd fixed its gaze on Bin Laden, a wave of contentment washed over him.

"Again, I knew you would respond as you did, my sons and sons of Allah, for you follow the teachings of Muhammad, the finest example of an honorable, righteous, and merciful man."

Suddenly, a speck appeared on one of the many mountain peaks around the wide, green plain. It grew into a sinister figure, that, in a voice like a storm wind roared, "Who do you think you are, you no account, who speak in my name and that of Allah! How dare you incite your followers to kill innocent people in the name of Allah, like those people today…."

Bin Laden froze.

"By distorting the teachings of Islam, which in other languages means peace and understanding, you have committed the worst crime imaginable. The destruction of the Twin Towers didn't bring peace to the world. You know Allah teaches us to do good and fight evil with every legal means: our hands, our words, and when necessary, swords and fire, but never by killing people who only dreamed of peace and happiness. Repent before it's too late, you traitor of Islam. Otherwise, Allah will kill you and your followers!"

Bin Laden, who had crouched on the ground, gazed upward, and to his relief, Muhammad had disappeared But he knew his shadow would haunt him until the day he died. He would not go to the heaven he had invented to convince his followers to sacrifice themselves.

Fatie's words stunned everyone. When she felt a gentle hand on her shoulder, she turned and saw Sokol.

"At first, I wanted to grill that narrow-minded businessman," he said, "but you put him in his place."

"I owed it to everyone here," said Fatie.

As she spoke, she saw Sokol's pale face.

"You don't look well," she said.

To be sure, he was wiped out.

"I know how you feel. Even though I've only been working here for about a year, I got to know those flight attendants. You knew them and the pilots even longer."

Sokol closed his eyes.

"Sit down. You need a break."

As he was walking toward a chair, Gary approached him.

"Congratulations," he said, forcing a smile. "You made Jay come to you and hang his head in shame."

Gary's words disgusted Sokol.

"I understand he apologized to you and said in light of what happened, he should have listened to you when you told him passengers should not be allowed to take pocket knives, bottles, or whatever else on board."

Sokol's eye's darkened. Then, he said in a mocking tone, "Weren't you the one who tried to stop me the day I was talking to Jay about that very issue? Weren't you the one who told me to mind my own business?"

"I didn't say that."

Gary moved his head in such a way he almost lost his glasses.

"You may not have said those exact words, but you implied them with your condescending tone."

Gary's eyes fluttered, and his nostrils twitched.

"Let bygones be bygones," he said with a yawned. "I plan to give you a raise. As you and other employees have pointed out, eight dollars an hour is too little for such a demanding job. I will discuss this matter with other company bosses. Just make sure we don't experience another disaster like this one. Are we done then?"

"No," said Sokol. "All you care about is making more and more money. You only hire seven or eight workers for your company's security checkpoints, not fourteen as the contract stipulates. People have quit because of the bad pay. You mainly hire Albanians because with their limited English, they won't complain. Isn't that so?"

Gary's face looked like that of a corpse. He kept silent.

"If the airlines had been more vigilant, your company would have lost this terminal, and you would have been charged with dereliction of duty."

Gary screwed up his face, but before he could respond, Sokol turned his back and sat in one of the chairs passengers usually sat in when waiting for their flights. He felt his conversation with Gary had been one of the many outrages he had experienced this day. He decided to look for another job. The TV continued to broadcast interviews with experts who tried to determine the cause of this tragedy. In the end, they suspected what everyone already knew: the terrorists had used knives and bottles. But they failed to mention that the FAA, FBI, and other government institutions were also responsible.

"I wonder what Steve's up to," Sokol said to himself.

He looked at his watch. It was 12:15. In just five hours, America had been turned on its head.

Sokol dialed Steve's cell, but hung up immediately. What words of comfort could he offer?

Steve entered the hall in the hotel where his wedding was supposed to have taken place. Suddenly, he heard Jacqueline's voice. Stunned, he turned and saw her and her family. She wore a white dress, and a veil covered her smiling, white face. She seemed to come from the land of bliss.

"I came back, Darling," she said, opening her arms.

Steve didn't know what to say. He was half dreaming, half awake, between the real and the surreal.

"Why are you surprised, Steve?" she asked. "Weren't you the one who lured me with our special song every time you threw your arms around me:

Honey, come back in September, the month we met.
Come back and let us run, hand in hand
Through the meadow and the forest?"

"I kept my promise," she added, a note of triumph in her voice.

Looking at Steve with tenderness, she continued to sing:

"I came back as promised, my darling,

In my wedding dress,
A bride in September with its twilight breezes
And rays of sparkling sunshine.
Therefore, say to our friends,
You are invited to our wedding."

At once, the hall was crowded with guests, among them, Besim and Marta who approached Steve and Jacqueline, lifted Jacqueline's veil, and began singing the Albanian song they had agreed to sing at their wedding:

"How beautiful is the bride,
As beautiful as beauty,
Her body like a cypress,
Eyes like an olive tree."

What a coincidence! Didn't that song describe Jacqueline? Wasn't she strong and graceful with eyes as dark as olives, unusual for someone with hair?

Steve reached for Jacqueline, pulled her to him, and kissed her. Meanwhile, the wedding guests sang songs from their countries of origin. Steve's boss sang Polish songs, Jim sang Scottish songs, a cameraman sang Hungarian songs, and Steve's driver sang Brazilian songs. The snippets of songs melded into an intoxicating poppourri. The guests danced the polka, the cardas, and the samba. Besim, Marta, Rrok, and Sokol, danced Albanian dances. Even Marko performed dances he had seen years ago in an Albanian documentary called Dances of the Eagles. It was the colorful choreography of America, which welcomed people from all over the world with open arms. Steve and Jacqueline also danced to the charming melodies.

"Mr. Ferguson?" said a voice behind Steve.

Steve whirled around and saw the hotel manager, who smiled nervously.

"I told you not to worry," he said. "We did everything you asked. You can see for yourself."

After a brief pause, he added, "But why didn't you bring Miss Cramer with you? She would have been pleased. We did everything she wanted, too."

The manager spoke with aloofness, as if he feared he was insulting Steve.

"You and Miss Cramer can come by any time. I'll be here."

His eyes shone as he continued, "You look upset. Is something wrong?"

Then, as if remembering something, his eyes widened, and he stammered, "How stupid of me! You witnessed the horror at the Twin Towers, and here I am bothering you with my chatter. Pull yourself together. Then we'll talk."

Embarrassed, the manager left the room.

A feeling of loneliness overcame Steve. The happiness of a few moments ago had been an illusion. He was alone in the hall through which people came and went, still dazed by the day's events. There were no wedding guests, and worst of all, Jacqueline was gone.

Steve went to a corner and slumped, exhausted, into a chair. To be sure, he needed to rest. The big man, who had patiently borne his suffering on television, shook with sobbs.

After a few minutes, Sokol, his heart pounding, called Steve's cell again and heard his distant, muffled voice.

"Oh, Steve, I don't know what to say," he stammered. "I'm a writer and a journalist like you, and words have never failed me until now. Your reports touched all of us. You not only expressed America's sorrow, but also the pain of losing Jacqueline. I could never have done what you did."

Sokol couldn't say any more. In fact, he felt as if he had said too much.

"That's not true," said Steve, trying to keep his composure. "You can do much more than I did. Since you witnessed these events, and since you worked with and befriended several of the victims, you should write a novel about them. Remember, just as the sly Greeks conquered Troy with a wooden horse, the devious terrorists destroyed the Twin Towers with planes. That should never have happened. Although the towers fell, America will never fall, but will remain the Promised Land for everyone in search of a better life. This makes us proud even as we mourn. You must write about the September 11 tragedy."

Sokol took Steve's words not as an order, but as a wish, a request, and a duty. Though his lips felt parched, he managed to say, "Thank you, my friend, for your suggestion. I promise I will write about today's tragedy."

Sokol hung up his phone and closed his eyes. He recalled his time working at Logan International Airport and his first meeting with the impish Jacqueline. He thought of Emma, a pleasant African-American woman with a splendid sense of humor, and Greta, who took her first and last flight. He thought of the pilots: Chris, who was about to start teaching at a flight school, and his young friend, Patrick, who admired him. Sokol had said good-bye to Emma, Greta, Chris, and Patrick as they took pictures with Jacqueline and promised to raise a toast on the plane in honor of her and Steve's wedding.

He thought of Besim and Rrok, who couldn't wait to go back to Kosovo and Gruda. He also recalled Marko's jokes. Finally, he thought of the terrorists, especially the one with the angelic face and the one who seemed to have languished for a long time. If only Sokol hadn't let them take the pocket knives and bottles on board, with which they committed one of the worst crimes in history!

He also thought of the feisty, elderly couple, George and Amanda, as well as the hundreds of people in the towers whom he hadn't known, yet felt as if he had known, whose lives, like those of his friends, had been cut short in brutal fashion. Although he was alone, he pictured Steve next to him and proclaimed, "My friend, I promise I will write about them!"

North Quincy, Boston, MA
February-August, 2008
January-March, 2016

ABOUT THE AUTHOR

Skifter Këllici was born in Tirana, Albania and received a diploma in history and literature from the University of Tirana. He worked as a journalist, scholar, and sportscaster on radio and television. He is the author of several novels and nonfiction books, including the children's books, "Memories of the Old Neighborhood" and "In the Footsteps" as well as the historical novels, "Assassination in Paris", "The Murderer with the White Hands", and "September Disaster." He wrote the screenplay for "In the Footsteps" which won a special prize at the International Children's Film Festival in Giffoni, Italy in 1979. He has lived in Boston, Massachusetts since 1999.

ABOUT THE TRANSLATOR

Carrie Hooper was born and raised in Elmira, New York. She has been blind since birth. She received a B.A. in vocal performance from Mansfield University, Mansfield, Pennsylvania. She went on to receive an M.A. in German and an M.A. in vocal performance from the State University of New York at Buffalo. After completing her studies, she spent a year at the Royal University College of Music in Stockholm, Sweden as a Fulbright scholar.

Carrie currently lives in Elmira, New York. She taught German, Italian, and Romanian at Elmira College. She has a passion for foreign languages and in addition to the languages mentioned above, she is also proficient in Swedish, Spanish, and Albanian. Music also plays an important role in Carrie's life. She teaches voice and piano lessons, gives vocal concerts, plays the piano and organ at a church, and sings in a community chorus.

Carrie not only loves music and languages, but also enjoys poetry. She has published three books: "Piktura në fjalë" ("Word Paintings"), a bilingual collection of poetry (Albanian-English), "My Life in My Words", and "Away from Home." She has also translated texts from Albanian and Romanian to English.

www.ingramcontent.com/pod-product-compliance
Ingram Content Group UK Ltd.
Pitfield, Milton Keynes, MK11 3LW, UK
UKHW020139250726
13967UKWH00002B/762

9 781794 751460